ANN RE

The Dance Card

PAGE PUBLISHING, INC.
New York, NY

First originally published by Page Publishing, Inc. 2015

ISBN 978-1-62838-641-7 (pbk)
ISBN 978-1-62838-642-4 (digital)
ISBN 978-1-62838-643-1 (hardcover)

Printed in the United States of America

Acknowledgements

For my two beautiful, supportive daughters, Natalie and Britta. Thank you for your continual encouragement and love.

For my four sisters who have shaped my life in so many positive ways through our friendship, fun, and crazy loving years growing old together: Sue, Priscilla, Mary, and Carol (who is guiding me from the heavens).

For the many friends, men and women, who have encouraged me and enhanced my life before and after a life changing event. Thank you Sally, Brenda, Doneta, and Kay.

Introduction

Without a hint of prior warning, in 2006, I found myself betrayed after 30 years of marriage. My husband announced he was leaving. He no longer loved me and wanted a divorce. The fabric of my family of four was now tattered; we were no longer whole. He was the father of my children , my confidant and best friend. That one individual I had dreamed of spending the rest of my life with.

That dream came to an unceremonious and unexpected end. It was a rude awakening. My life upended, I was forced into an unexpected situation in my life, one that completely shattered my dreams of eternal marital bliss. No one could ever understand what I was going through, nor did they care, or so I thought.

What I came to understand is that many men as well as women representing all economic, educational and social levels struggle with the end of their marital dreams of living happily ever after, trying to comprehend what went wrong in their marriages, coping with the anger, despair and heartache that often afflicts the spouse left behind, who has to learn to live on one's own. Starting over after living a shared life with a marital spouse or partner can be challenging, unnerving, and often lonely. But it doesn't have to be. Jumping into the single scene after many years of marriage can be daunting, intimidating, humiliating, and an affront to one's self esteem but it can also be fun, enriching, and an antidote to loneliness.

Instead of hanging my head low, at age 56 I jumped into the deep end of cyberspace dating pool. My suitors? Based on their expression of style and the nature of their "game", I awarded these "gents" alter ego names tied to a particular dance such as Mr. Rumba and Mr. Slow dance, Mr Jitterbug and Mr. Waltz.

During my seven-year search for romance and happiness, I discovered much about myself and uncovered many helpful clues for managing and nurturing relationships. It is my hope that my journey on the road after divorce will help others find comfort after the dissolution of a marriage.

When life offers us a challenge, we can choose to cave in or respond to that challenge in ways that will make us grow. I hope that my story will inspire divorced and widowed readers that there is romance out there for everyone at any age after the end of a marriage.

The characters in this novel are fictitious.
Any resemblance to actual events or individuals
is entirely coincidental.

Preface

The story is familiar. A long-term relationship dissolves. Onetime partners in life become disconnected, forcing each into unexpected changes in the dance of love, life, and relationships. Meeting a new prospective dance partner requires looking to our laptops to learn the art of dating in cyberspace. Dance is an expressive form of art, and the art of dating is a beautiful form of dance. The many personalities become specific dances, each one bringing different and varied moves to the dance floor of love. Finding that perfect partner—on and off the dance floor—becomes an exciting, romantic, sensual, and humorous experience. Filling out a dance card is the beginning of an introspective and enlightening journey—one that is still a work in progress.

Chapter 1

September ninth was a night of unexpected consolation. It began with a frantic phone call from a dear friend of 30 years. Her speech was nearly inaudible through gasps and intermittent sobbing. "Annie, what am I going to do? What am I going to do?"

"Is everything all right? Talk to me."

There was a pause, and then a whisper of garbled words replied, "Can you come over? I need to talk to someone. It's awful. I can't believe what's happening. Please, I need you. I need someone to talk to. You're the only one I can talk to right now. You were the first person I called."

"Yes, yes, of course, I'll be right over. Be there in 10 minutes. Please try to calm down. Everything will be all right, my dear friend."

My first thought was that someone was hurt, so I jumped into my car and proceeded down the road to my distraught friend's home. The multitude of thoughts that swirled in my head was frightening. What was happening? Was it something serious? Was someone hurt? How was I going to help in this situation? My mind felt like a machine in full operational mode, with the problem solving mechanism in high gear. I would solve the problem, no matter the issue.

As I approached the dark entryway, I noticed the room was void of its usual happy and electric atmosphere. The family filled with energy and love was no longer present. Appearing distraught, eyes swollen and filled with grief, my friend was inconsolable.

"He left. I came home, and there was a note right there," she said, as she gestured toward the ledge of the stairway.

"He said he was done and didn't love me anymore, and wanted to find the happiness he deserves. He blindsided me and packed up all of his belongings and left. I don't know where he is, what he's doing, or who he's with. He was my best friend. I was his best friend. How can someone do this? How am I going to go on without him? I want to die."

Immediately the past six years of my life came flooding back in a fury of emotions. It had been almost six years to this day that the man I called my life partner, lover, husband, and the father of my two beautiful teenage daughters said those exact words: "I have lost all romantic feelings for you and want to find someone who can share those feelings with me." He was 55-years-old and when he left, the life we built together over 30 years was thrown out as if it had never existed. The pieces of our spoiled relationship were discarded like trash left for the scavengers to pick up, to devour or spit out. Those haunting words, "*I don't love you anymore*," had stayed with me.

I was forced into an unexpected situation in my life, one that completely shattered my dreams of eternal married bliss. The ultimate perfect family was exposed as nothing more than a charade we played; we were actors playing our respective roles on different stages, only to go home after rehearsal to play very different roles. My partner and husband had reached a plateau in his life, and decided to leave this charade to search for happiness in some other form on a new stage.

As I comforted my friend, my own defining moment was vividly clear in my mind. As a mother and caretaker, my protective and survival instincts kicked in. I needed to fight and protect my wonder family of four. At that moment of initial shock, my naïve brain said that none of this was real. This was but a momentary lapse of clear judgment on the part of this man who I thought I knew. He was just beginning his long-awaited retirement from a very stressful and time-consuming position as a corporate executive. We were supposed to be entering into a less stressful stage of life, and the possibilities were new and exciting. Thinking this was a temporary setback, I was ready to tackle the problem head on. I was the fixer, the director, the CEO of the family. I felt everything would be all right. I would undo all that had been damaged emotionally and functionally. We would get through this.

Alas, we didn't. He was already gone, out the marital door, and had been, in his struggling mind, for months if not years before that day. I was clueless. The signs may have been there, but they were either misinterpreted or ignored. I was alone. In my mind and new world, I felt that I was the only one ever to experience this pain of loss and confusion. This profound, uncontrollable grief encompassed so much more than the man himself—my best friend and confidant, lover, provider, and father of my children. No one could ever understand what I was going through or cared, or so I *thought*. I went through loss, sadness, anger, confusion, depression, and disbelief.

My initial thoughts focused on our children, the embodiment of our relationship. The kids, albeit young adults now, would always be considered merely collateral damage to those not immediately involved, but they too would feel the pain and grief of separation and loss. Divorce's effects on children seem to be forgotten by those who, in their selfish lapses of judgment, do not see that their actions turn what was once whole into pieces. When the whole is no longer intact, efforts to maintain a family unit through events such as graduations, marriages, and the arrival of grandchildren will be strained. I wondered if, in the years to come, my ex-husband would show a little remorse for the effects of his actions on the many people who were left behind—not only the immediate family, but also all the people he called family for so many years. Even people on the outside of a long-term relationship are affected in one way or another by its dissolution. The collateral damage is indescribable..

It had been the six years since my husband had left me and our family, and in those six long years I had discovered that what happened to us was not an isolated phenomenon. This moment with my friend was a reminder of my own inconsolable days and nights of sadness and hopelessness, but it was only the most recent reminder; I was reliving the dance of grief with so many of my close contemporaries, both female and male friends. Their stories are so similar in many ways: people in long-term marriages with two or more children, successful in life, and financially secure, respected in the community— but all discontented with themselves and the lives they created, hoping to find that ultimate happiness in their disjointed minds for the third or fourth quarter of their lives. These people seemed eager to dance away from marital commitments that must have felt distant, since they acted with little or with no regard for the long-term consequences.

I knew that I could show my dear friend both care and sympathy, something that I had never received during my own worst moments from those who knew me. It was understandable because one cannot give support when one has little first-hand knowledge of this kind of situation, and when two parties, both friends, are involved. I did not want this for my friend. I knew all too well what she would endure, and wanted to help her through this period of disruption in her once happy life. It was evident that she was experiencing shock and confusion. There were no immediate solutions at this point; only time would allow her to verbalize the pain, which amounted to an acute situational depression. Rationalizing and forming a plan of action were not appropriate then, but in the back of my mind I was thinking about how to proceed. I knew what to expect, having experienced all the stages of this grief process; it was painful, but the stages of grief led me to become a healthier whole, to resolve those painful moments, and to move forward in a positive way. The gamut of emotions has to occur for anyone to cope with a loss of a loved one. I could. only help my friend through this process step by step. Listening was my first objective; I needed to allow her to verbalize all that she was feeling.

As I listened, the words and the story become all too familiar. There was an affair years ago, and one or both could not get past the betrayal and feelings of guilt that result when a partner has been unfaithful. The trust issue became tantamount, and even though the couple underwent extensive therapy, it never resolved that feeling of deception and distrust. The ability to maintain a partnership of two is like any form of dancing—we must understand the need to practice as one unit. The dance of life and love is a collaboration of trust, understanding, and desire.

As I heard my friend's story, it occurred to me that monogamy seems to be the exception, rather than the norm. Too many individual men and women need multiple partners to feel a sense of longing, or love if you will, or need, from their own partners. There is no specific time when relationships turn stale and crumble both emotionally and sexually, when stimulation is sought elsewhere. In both my friend's case and my own, our partners left after rationalizing that the people they married had become too familiar and less exciting; they felt they deserved another chance at happiness with a new partner. Maybe we lost that appeal that was present long ago; maybe our spouses felt that we were not as attractive as we once were, or just felt bored living with people with whom they'd lost their connections. Two lives became disjointed as priorities changed with age and time.

I had heard it before. The breadwinner whose task is to provide for a growing family financially gets caught up in a separate idealized corporate world, prioritizing the home life to a secondary concern. This kind of thinking only creates a distance between two dancers. Their footing becomes unbalanced, as does their connection in the relationship world. They become dancers moving to a completely different rhythm. It is time to throw out the old dance shoes, and begin a new set of dance steps for the last quarter of their lives.

The helplessness one feels when a marriage dissolves is indescribable. No one else can ever know what this feels like. One imagines every other couple lives in a fantasy world of love and romance and butterflies and fireworks after years together. I remember thinking that I would not wish this on anyone.

"Why is my marriage so different? What did I do wrong?" my friend asked.

Invariably, neither party did anything wrong; dissatisfaction from either one made for dissatisfaction in the other. Resentment set in, and the once-unified couple became enemies to themselves. Inconceivable, really, that a loving and compatible union can turn into a war zone, and yet alliances change and defense mechanisms arise. The fact of the matter is that one in two marriages ultimately dissolve, and statistically, the likelihood becomes greater with the acceptance of divorce, which is symptomatic of the commonplace laissez faire attitude that, these days, accompanies commitment, communication, and caring for individuals.

Since my divorce, I have played counselor and psychotherapist to many of my dear friends, men and women, who have faced the ends of their marriages. Most ended in divorce, and not on a positive note. Each endured the stages of grief, all in differing order, and in different ways. There is no right way to experience grief, and to say there is a right way or wrong way would be to minimize the pain and loss of divorce. I knew how frustrated my friends felt, knowing that they would be left alone, not knowing who to turn to, or how to deal with helping their children get through this situation. The drama and the damage are done, and there is no turning back.

After my own divorce and the divorces of so many friends, I began to question the feasibility of long-term monogamous relationships and the oncecherished 1950s *Leave It to Beaver* loving nuclear family, the one that's supposed to last for the rest of our lives, happy as a whole. This is a new and more impersonal era, one of selfishness, less caring toward our fellow humans. We live in a throwaway society. Everything has become disposable: the food we eat, the clothes we wear, the homes we live in, the cars we drive. All can be replaced by something new and different, a quick fix, another high to feed our addicted, self-serving souls. Disposing of lives has become easy and commonplace too. We discard relationships without regard for those who we once thought were so important in our lives. Done, thrown away. No use for them anymore. They served their purpose, and so it's time to find another unsuspecting sucker to replace the old. This is the pattern.

The dance of life and love is a continuum, though, and for every stumble, there's a chance to stand up and start again. My dance of life continues, and I knew that September night that after many years of reflection that led to acceptance, and even contentment, with this enormous change, it was time to move forward to a happier and more fulfilling place in my mind and spirit.

I became curious about life outside the world of couple-dom. I ventured out to see if other relationships followed patterns similar to those that I had experienced. Are we a small minority in an elite group of over-achievers and high achievers who need constant gratification to feel good about ourselves, or does the human race as a whole act in the same way?

After six years and a lot of courage, my heart and brain said, *Let's explore the singles scene.* But where does a fifty-plus-something woman with grown children who hasn't dated in 30 years begin?

Ah, the Internet. There are so many sites out there now, and the advertising is ubiquitous on the computer, television, and radio. We are bombarded by pop-up ads for Eharmony. com, Match.com, Single Seniors, Faith in Relationships, Asian Singles, Plenty of Fish, It's Just Lunch, Zoosk, OurTime, OkCupid, and even more sites. The more they advertise, the more the response and demand for the product, so there must be many people on these sites.

One site in particular caught my attention, so I visited it. Shock does not describe the feeling I had when I clicked that mouse. I began perusing the number of men and women looking for love. Where were all these people coming from? What were their stories, and why had they reached the same point I had? My curiosity began to flicker. But before actually signing up for the site, I decided to explore the many eligible bachelors and read a little about them.

Profiles give a brief synopsis of a person's background and interests. Information including likes, political affiliation, educational background, heritage, and physical attributes like height, weight, and hair color is available. Then there's the all-important profile picture, which catches the eye initially, and if you're lucky, the profile includes a few more pictures. The profile picture can be a deal breaker from the start, but any picture is better than no picture at all. Why? Well, that is the six-million-dollar question. If a person doesn't post a picture, it stands to reason that he is either unattractive or has 13 heads, which will never get a response. If you're less shallow than the average person, and allow yourself to read profiles without pictures without judging them, perhaps you might find someone interesting, and request a photo. As for me, I might love what is written, but if the picture doesn't match the profile or my ideal, then there will be no possibility of continuing the communication. Sad, but true.

Let the dance begin! "New to this kind of dating," I cleverly stated in my profile introduction. Of course, nearly everyone else on these Internet sites is new to this kind of dating, or why else would they be there? Gone are the days of blind dates set up by a friend, or meeting at a local church, or barhopping, or even looking for love in the produce or dairy section of the local grocery store. For me, online dating felt especially new after 30 years of being in a monogamous relationship; dating now is quite different from the dating of the '50s and '60s.

Back then, the ideal outcome for a couple's first date would find June Cleaver in a cinched waist dress donning a freshly ironed apron, cleaning her spotless home while waiting for Ward to come home from a long day's work. He'd sit in his appointed comfy chair reading his daily newspaper, waiting for his home-cooked meal. It was a simpler time but one of true, committed relationships between a man and woman—or so it would seem. Are those days forever gone? I soon discovered that the ideal remained, even if the reality didn't.

Meeting a prospective partner is quite different from the days of flirting across the gymnasium floor at our local recreational centers where the school or community dances were held. I remember holding that cardboard dance card with names of all the boys listed from 1 to 10 next to the song or dance that they had claimed. Looking over the names on the dance card was always thrilling. There was always that one person who gave me butterflies when I anticipated walking across that highly polished gymnasium wood floor, arms outstretched to be taken into the embrace of that special person and held close for that long-awaited slow dance, or to be swung around and dipped during the faster, more energetic dances. Were those same youthful feelings of excitement at all possible again? Would that possible partner in my dance of life have reciprocal feelings? Could it lead to a long-term partner for friendship or an intimate relationship? The potential dance partners were endless, as I soon discovered once I perused these sites for names to add to my dance card. Maybe there would be that one dance partner to sweep me off my feet as I once felt when I was a girl. Which number and which dance would he be?

The newly made dance card proved to be a lesson in the differences between men and women with regard to how we experience similar situations differently when it comes to relationships. I learned from all of my dates, each of whom I named after a different dance, that life experiences form a person and that person's interests, just as educational background and family history also affect how we each approach a potential partner in this dance of life. These lessons continue to intrigue me, and each date proved to be a new and interesting form of dance between two people.

Let me begin by describing how Internet dating works. One of my earliest dance partners described the online dating experience as being in a store window, naked, exposed to all potential shoppers for goods that they may want to purchase.

Not every item is desirable; in fact, very few of the items on our grocery list are desirable at all.

We have all become particular about the goods we look for and will not settle for anything that is damaged in our eyes. As we are mature and have differing experiences, we become more selective about whom we may want to dance with. No one wants to settle for less than they think they deserve or feel they may be compatible with; no one wants to settle for the sake of settling. I cannot tell you how many men have given me that line during our dates. It's as if all the men on these sites have spoken to one another and advised each other not to "settle for settling's sake." I understand the need to be selective. It occurred to me to consider that if we had selected properly the first time around when it came to marriage, we wouldn't be in the position of searching for a new dance partner. But I rejected that kind of thinking, because most likely the same situation would have played out the same way no matter who I started dancing with in the beginning.

Another dance partner equated dating online to being in a used car lot and choosing the one that would catch someone's eye, the sleek look of the exterior as well as the fit while sliding into that front seat. Would the ride be perfect if there were the bumps along the rocky road of discovery? Would this car be able to handle the remaining years together like a racing team riding the road of life? I wasn't able to identify with this comparison, describing a car as a partner in love and life; I thought how silly. It also was a reminder of how easily one traded in automobiles when a new model became available. Once again, easily discarded.

My quest to find potential dates seemed overwhelming at first. I decided to start by seeing who was out there and available. I was curious to learn more about my potential dance partners' differing personalities, where their lives started, where the years had taken them, and why they ended up on the dating site, like I did. What were their expectations for a woman? Would they be interested in developing a long-term relationship, or were they only looking for friendship?

The answers, I found out, were as varied as the men themselves. Every man had a unique personality, which I found myself associating with different types of dance. I chose dances to describe the men that I have become acquainted with because they all came to the first date with completely different moves.

Dance is a vibrant and extremely expressive form of art, with both aesthetic and social components. Any and all forms of dance have the power to bind people together on an emotional level, in romance or in friendship. The art of dating is like a beautiful form of dance, providing social and intimate interaction between two people. The rhythm of the music allows for individual interpretation and for two people to improvise dance steps as they start dating. Some who take those first dance steps successfully complete their dance, and some falter, stumbling over their own feet....

Ballroom dancing has become one of the most entertaining and popular styles of dance, especially with the success of the reality shows *Dancing with the Stars* and *So You Think You Can Dance*. I discovered there are quite a few gentlemen who watch that show, and we have shared many conversations about who and what dance routines we favored. Ballroom used to be for only the privileged class, but today, the popularity transcends all classes.

Every dance form has its own unique identity, just like a person. Each person and each dance is beautiful and appealing in its own way. As I started dating again, I found that the men I dated reminded me of different dances, the movements of the dances reflecting their personalities. Here are some of the dances that came to mind when I started dating:

The Contemporary Dance: An artistic dance with a high level of difficulty. This is an aspiring dance, with its own form of expression through improvisation.

The Slow Dance: A partner dance in which the dancers sway to slow music. It is a simple dance, usually performed by middle school or high school students. The foot movement is minimal, requiring little concentration.

The Tango: They say "it takes two to tango," but in this form of ballroom dance, the man definitely leads the woman. The moves are masculine and sensual at the same time. I find the dominance of the male partner in guiding his female partner through the beautiful, elegant, and flowing steps to be very pleasant. The partners embrace and focus on each other. The tango is a social dance, more improvised, with each step spontaneous. The steps are rhythmic and regular, but there are a variety of patterns. The manner in which the steps are executed is important because to dance successfully, the partners must pay particular attention to each other, creating the electric connection we expect from the tango.

The Waltz: The waltz is a slower form of ballroom dance. The beat of the music is slow and rhythmic, and the partners perform close together, as if they were attached at the upper torso.

The Cha-cha-cha: Originating from Cuban dance, the cha-cha-cha is rhythmic and energetic, with slow movements as well.

The Rumba: A syncopated musical dance in double time, which originated in Cuba. It features a complex footwork and violent movements. The slow rhythm of the hip movements is coordinated and is beautifully romantic and sensual. The woman seductively moves her body, holding the ends of her skirt, opening and closing the skirt with the rhythm of the music. The man distracts his partner, surprising her with erotic movements; a single pelvic thrust symbolizes sexual penetration. The woman closes her skirt to cover the area being attacked, blocking the thrust.

The Salsa: A very flirtatious dance of Latin American origin. The basic footwork is similar to the rumba; the steps are quick forward and backward movements. The woman has to mirror the steps of the man. It requires perfect coordination and a high level of chemistry to perform steamy sultry numbers.

The Jive: This lively variation of the jitterbug, a faster version of the swing dance, is one of the five international Latin dances. It is energetic, featuring kicks and bounces mostly with the balls of the dancer's feet. The jitterbug's frenetic moves lift the spirits. Its name comes from alcoholics suffering from the "jitters" (delirium tremors), dancing without control or understanding of the movements, jumping around and going crazy.

The Country/Western Two-Step: The two-step moves counterclockwise around the dance floor. The leader, usually the man, determines the movements. The partners dance facing each other in either a closed or an open position. The man holds the woman's right hand in his left hand while his right hand is on the left shoulder of his partner. The steps come in threes: a quick step, another quick step, and then a slow step. A smooth and gliding movement in time with the music is desirable. The two-step is a fun and bouncy dance.

The Grind: Inhibitions are all removed. If a dancer is a little inhibited or shy, this is a wonderful dance to melt that ice when meeting someone for the first time. Facing in the same direction, one dancer's groin should be in contact with the other's behind, or, alternatively, the pair faces each other with hips aligned; the partners rub together in a seductive groove. They bend their knees, swaying rhythmically along with the music. Grinding is also commonly referred to as freak dancing or freaking.

Together, these dances made up my dance card. I was ready for the dances to begin, and wondered who would be left standing. The match dance begins with willingness to expose oneself out in cyber land, to be viewed, scrutinized, admired, criticized, and fantasized about. Even though I was at an age when fears seemed to dissipate, and even though I had been blessed with life's experience, curiosity, and excitement, I still wondered if anyone out there would find me interesting, attractive, and desirable.

Nevertheless, I put my hesitations aside. My emotionally charged mind had finally reached the point of acceptance: it was time to move forward. I felt a confidence that was missing from my inner being for so many years. I felt I was deserving of recognition, respect, honor, love, and all that goes along with finding the right partner in dance and in life. And besides, I hoped that my experiences would help those who were also forced to start over in middle life.

First, I had to overcome my fears and insecurity about being judged according to the media's unrealistic standards of female attractiveness. I knew that I was no longer a young woman, but I didn't let that stop me: if you are not eager to begin again, then you are not ready to ask someone to join you for that first dance.

With so many dating websites to choose from, it was difficult to decide which one was right for me. When I first started thinking about online dating, I asked my adult niece to look first and assess what was out there. As a young twenty-something woman with a little experience in the dating world, she was eager to assist me with my moving on in life.

"Auntie, you are youthful and so vivacious. You deserve to have the best that life has to offer. You have been an important part in my life and I want to see you happy," she said.

Ah! What an affirmation from a loved one as I began this process!

"How do I begin? Do you have any idea how any of this works?" Not being too savvy about the technological advances of today's society, it was a good thing that she was there to help. The younger generation has grown up with computers, cell phones, texting, and social media: Twitter, Tumblr, Facebook, Instagram, and the like. Our communications are continuous, and the need and desire to connect in the digital world is part of our daily regimen. From where I stand, digital connections are compressed, usually without depth, and generally lack meaning or substance, especially compared to an in-person connection. And yet there I was, about to start the investigation of love and future dance partners online.

As I learned, when you visit a site, you enter an e-mail address. The site will prompt you to fill in who are you looking for in terms of gender, age, demographics, and distance—10 miles or 10,000 miles from your zip code? With the touch of the finger, pages upon pages of pictures appear. Usually sites show 25 pictures on a page so as not to overwhelm you, but there may be hundreds of pages depending on the criteria selected. You may browse the listed individuals and read what they have to say. If you are not a member, you are unable to contact anyone or communicate via the secure site. Of course, looking for free stimulates you to join the site officially once you see someone you are attracted to and want to contact.

Before I joined, I reflected on what I was hoping to gain from this process. I must say that I was not desperately looking for someone to fill a void in my life, nor was I thinking of finding a long-term partner or a potential husband. I was not at that stage and was not sure if I ever would be again, quite frankly. I wanted to meet new people with similar experiences and enjoy their company for an evening or two; I was looking forward to companionship for dining, seeing a movie, going to a sporting event, and, of course, dancing. "Needy" and "desperate" are not words anyone would use to describe me. I later found that many others were quite the opposite; the need, not just the desire, to settle down was the first and foremost item on the agenda for the vast majority of the men I connected with. Others, I must admit, were cautious and played games.

Sitting at my desk, in the home that was once filled with my family of four, I could only imagine what my life would be like in the near future. Joining an Internet dating site was the beginning of an experiment and experience I would take with me, and hopefully, it would help others through a painful time in their lives and show them that we are not alone in this rebuilding of our lives.

I decided on a prominent, well-advertised site to join. I chose to sign up for a month of eligibility. The first step was to set up my own individual profile and username, something catchy and descriptive at the same time. Coming up with a username is harder than you might think.

"Why not your nickname, Auntie?"

"Cute idea, but maybe not catchy enough," I said. You could try to use your first name, but chances are that others have already used it, so the site will prompt you with other possible names that haven't been used.

"Hot Babe in Need of a Dance Partner."

"Oh, I don't think that's classy."

"'How about 'Looking for Love in All the Wrong Places'?"

"Ooh, I am really not looking for love and that's corny."

"Lost Dance Partner?"

All this was becoming too much of a task, so I submitted my first name, something I could remember, and up popped Annie14Bunny. Hm. Interesting. My first name is Annie. My birthday is on the fourteenth, and my mother's nickname is Bunny. So there it was, perfect in my eyes.

Questions followed, all designed to provide my potential dance partners with as much information as possible. I was asked about my appearance, birth date, height, body type (athletic, toned, slim, slightly overweight), ethnicity, if had kids or wanted kids, relationship status (divorced, separated, widowed, never married), where I resided, occupation, smoking and drinking habits, income, background, values, faith, languages, education, heritage, and religious affiliation. Yet another line asked me about my interests, exercise habits, political views, pets, astrological sign, and favorite things to do and read. I provided enough data to start a memoir for sure.

I described myself to my best ability, and then described what I was looking for in the opposite sex. I answered all the questions asked of me. At this point, I began to evaluate all those specifics about past relationships I had experienced, and I realized I had never thought about any of these specific qualifications before choosing a partner in the past. It was apparent to me now that with age does come wisdom. When I was a young impressionable person, we didn't have enough life experience to qualitatively analyze the future with someone; maybe this new generation has the right idea. When I was young and vulnerable and naïve, the excitement that preceded a new love interest, especially the first love interest, easily overrode objective questions about compatibility. As we age and become more familiar with our own personal patterns in our experiences of finding a partner, the process is quite different; we see the dating process in a whole new light.

The most important part of the profile component of this game, or dance, of matches is the description, that well-thought-out paragraph pertaining to how you see yourself and how you want others to see you. When the site prompted me to describe myself, I once again enlisted my niece's assistance.

"You need to talk about all those fantastic things that interest you. You have so many talents, and now is the time to share with all those guys out there who don't even know you exist."

I remembered the years of being stifled and looked at as only someone's wife. I felt as if I lost my own identity. I was just a cast member in the ensemble of family life, standing obediently in the wings, supporting and nurturing the whole production with little or no recognition, no applause, no ovation, no expectation of being put on a pedestal and seen for myself. Now was the time to reclaim my individuality, and my abilities that had been overlooked over the years. Time to dance like no one is watching! Thanks to my lovely niece, I took hold of my courage and decided to give up my understudy's role, and become the lead on this new stage. My profile read, in all caps:

> I AM YOUTHFUL, SPIRITED, ROMANTIC, AND CARING, WITH A SENSITIVE AND INTROSPECTIVE HEART AND SOUL. I AM A LOVER OF NATURE AND LIFE.
>
> I AM LIBERAL, OPEN MINDED, AND FUN LOVING, WITH A SPIRIT EAGER FOR NEW ADVENTURES. I AM ATHLETIC, QUIET, AND RESERVED IN MOST SITUATIONS. I'M ADORING, NOT SELF-ABSORBED, BUT CONFIDENT IN MYSELF AND IN MY ABILITIES.
>
> MY HOPES AND DREAMS CENTER ON A SOUND VALUE SYSTEM, ONE THAT HONORS MY FAMILY AND PRIORITIZES THEIR NEEDS.

I AM A PARENT, DAUGHTER, SISTER, AUNT, AND FRIEND. I GENUINELY CARE ABOUT OTHERS AND LOOK FOR THE GOODNESS THAT WE ALL POSSESS.

PEOPLE SAY THAT I AM QUIET AND RESERVED, BUT CLASSY. I AM COMFORTABLE IN ALL SITUATIONS BUT PREFER SMALLER, MORE INTIMATE GATHERINGS. ATHLETICS ARE IMPORTANT TO ME AND KEEP ME STIMU- LATED IN BOTH MIND AND BODY. I CAN HIT A BASEBALL, THROW A SPIRAL, AND SWING A GOLF CLUB WITH THE BEST OF THEM, BUT MY FAVORITE SPORT IS TENNIS. I HAVE AN ENDURING LOVE FOR THE WATER, AND BEING ON A LAKE IN THE NORTH WOODS NURTURES MY SOUL.

I WILL ALWAYS EMBRACE THE NEEDY, AND I TREAT ALL PEOPLE WITH RESPECT, REGARDLESS OF THEIR CHALLENGES. I AM A REGISTERED NURSE, AND MY PROFESSION HAS TAUGHT ME TO APPRECIATE THE STRUG- GLES OTHERS HAVE ENDURED. I NEVER TAKE ANYTHING FOR GRANTED AND I TRY TO LIVE EACH DAY AS IF IT WERE MY LAST.

SOMETIMES PEOPLE COME INTO YOUR LIFE AND YOU KNOW RIGHT AWAY THAT THEY WERE MEANT TO BE THERE. THEY TEACH YOU A LESSON OR HELP YOU TO FIG- URE OUT WHO YOU ARE OR WHO YOU WANT TO BECOME. I AM HOPEFUL THAT THIS WILL HAPPEN FOR EVERYONE, NOT JUST FOR ME BUT FOR YOU AS WELL.

MY MATCH SHOULD LOVE TO GO OUT TO THE THEATRE AND TO CONCERTS (JAZZ, ROCK, SOUL). AS A PERFORMER WHO LOVES TO SING, IT'S IMPORTANT TO ME TO FIND SOMEONE WHO CAN APPRECIATE THIS PART OF MY LIFE. I ALSO LOVE SHOPPING, VISITING ART GALLERIES, TRAVELING TO METROPOLITAN CITIES, AND BROWSING ANTIQUE SHOPS IN REMOTE PLACES.

I HAVE LIVED ON BOTH COASTS AND HAVE FAMILY ALL OVER THE COUNTRY. THE MIDWEST HAS BEEN MY HOME FOR OVER THIRTY YEARS, AND MY ROOTS ARE HERE. HOWEVER, I AM FLEXIBLE AND COULD SEE MYSELF RELOCATING SOMEWHERE WARM.

I HAVE TWO WONDERFUL AND BEAUTIFUL ADULT DAUGHTERS WHO ARE MY WORLD. THEY ARE ON THEIR OWN NOW, AND I'M LOOKING FORWARD TO THIS NEW TIME TO EXPAND MY OWN HORIZONS. I HAVE A LOT MORE TO GIVE IN THESE NEXT YEARS OF MY LIFE. I WANT SOMEONE WHO WILL APPRECIATE ME FOR ME, AND ALL THAT I HAVE TO OFFER. MY IDEAL MATCH MUST RESPECT MY INDEPENDENCE, BUT ALSO NURTURE A FRIENDSHIP, WHICH REQUIRES THE GIVE AND TAKE THAT IS SO IMPORTANT IN A LOVING AND BALANCED RELATIONSHIP. I GUESS I AM GETTING A BIT TOO SERIOUS HERE, SO LET'S NOT FORGET THE IMPORTANCE OF FUN AND LAUGHTER!

I HAVE FOUR BROTHERS AND FOUR SISTERS, SO AS YOU CAN IMAGINE, I CAN ENDURE A LOT OF SPIRITED PLAY, AND I

LOVE A GOOD JOKE (YOU'LL OFTEN FIND ME
TELLING THEM!).

I LOVE TO TRAVEL AND EXPECT TO DO
MORE NOW, AND I THINK IT WOULD BE SO
MUCH MORE FUN WITH SOMEONE TO SHARE
THE MOMENTS WITH. I'M NOT SEARCHING
FOR A LONG-TERM COMMITMENT RIGHT
NOW, BUT I'M WILLING TO SEE WHAT LIFE
HAS IN STORE FOR ME, AND LEAVE THE DOOR
OPEN TO LET THE SUNSHINE IN.

After completing my personal profile, I was available for the picking. I felt exposed, with my personal information available to be viewed, scrutinized, admired, criticized, and fantasized about, much like a playmate on the cover of those scandalous magazines that boys used to hide in their bedrooms.

On the other hand, I figured that at my age, the fears should be lessened, and apprehensions diminished. Life experience makes us smarter about people, and gives us the ability to handle crises and stresses more calmly than we did when we were younger. Nothing ventured, nothing gained, as they say. I approached the online dating adventure pragmatically: if something happened, great, but if not, that would be acceptable too. I have always been a big proponent of enjoying the process of things, rather than counting on the end product. If you always focus on your journey's destination, once you get there you'll just be looking for the next stimuli.

After my I wrote my profile, the next step in the signup process was to describe what I was looking for in a perfect match. What kinds of qualities would best suit my desires? I had to decide if education was an important qualification, for example. Did I want my dancing partner to be an athlete? A laborer? An artist? What would my priorities tell me about myself?

Some people do not really have an idea of what they are looking for in a partner, and others are quite clear as to what may interest them. I'm one of the latter; I found it easy to list my preferences. Curiously, one of my first prerequisites for a potential dance partner was that he be tall. The other qualities I was looking for were important, but not deal breakers. I wanted a potential partner to be educated, honest, respectful, athletic, funny, and romantic. I later discovered another very important attribute: I wanted his family to be important to him, or at least his children. Knowing that a person had experienced the joys and difficulties in raising children would give us common ground, since we could share experiences regarding the fascination and stresses that go along with parenting.

Age and location were my last demographics to consider. I listed my age preference as 50 years to 60, and my geographic range within a 500-mile radius.

Now it was time to submit that last required item to stimulate the senses of all those men out there who are totally visual in nature—the photograph. The photo is probably the most important part of your dating profile, because it's the first thing that catches the eye. The dating website I used advises users to choose a shot that is casual yet semiformal, a headshot without external stimuli like a pet or landscape to distract potential partners. I wanted a photo that would show the real me, but perhaps the real me from the most flattering angle; after all, the profile photo is meant to catch other people's attention! After perusing my photo gallery, I decided on a classy, somewhat formal, head shot of myself in a little black dress and pearls.

I uploaded the photo and clicked "Finished." Instantly, before my eyes, a page of men's profiles appeared, profiles chosen because they matched my criteria. I perused photos, headlines, and profile snippets geared to catch my eye. With a click of the mouse, I could see a person's heart and soul poured out onto the virtual page in front of me. Profile pictures and headlines are like bait; it's the profile that's meant to reel a potential partner in, as I knew from writing my own profile.

The next step in playing the dating game usually begins with a notification that ones profile was viewed. No formal communication is in order; it is the first indication that one is interested. If the recipient seems at all interesting in terms of that person's looks or what they have written in their profiles, then the next move is yours—either a return click on their profile or a brief hello typed in the secure messaging center that the site provides.

As I started browsing through profiles, I felt a sense of fear, excitement, energy, and guilt. Because I had been in a committed relationship for so many years, looking for new companionship felt almost like a betrayal of the one I had loved and built a life with for so many years. I knew that I wasn't being unfaithful, but it still felt strange to know that I was free to be and do as I wanted without repercussions from anyone. And so for the following three hours, I sat at my computer perusing pages and pages of pictures and profiles—350 profiles, to be exact, on just that first day. Glancing quickly over the photos posted, I found it interesting how easy it was to eliminate those that did not strike my fancy, and how easy it was to pick out the very few that popped out at me as potential dates. Those that chose to not post a picture were quickly eliminated, narrowing down the playing field.

What shocked me the most as I scrolled was the sheer number of fifty-something men on the site; I hadn't expected so many. Most were recently divorced or separated, looking for that special someone to call the love of their lives. This was a recurring sentiment. Reading further, many of the men looking for long-term relationships had two or more children and were coming out of long marriages. A man like this wanted that perfect woman, someone to replace his wife, the woman who bore his child, supported his professional career, raised and created a family but maybe became bored with the humdrum daily grind of life. These men usually described themselves as handsome, sensitive, positive, successful, surrounded by family and friends, happy with their work, and financially secure. They claimed to want romance and tenderness, to love massages and thunderstorms. A typical profile might read, "loves holding hands and the simple pleasures of life" or, "if you like to be pampered and treated like a lady, please get in touch."

As I read over these kinds of profiles, one thing kept forcing itself into my mind. I did believe most of these guys wanted romance and love, but what I kept reading was *sex, sex, sex.* The woman these men want has to be sexually stimulating in the bedroom. Why? Bottom line: men, no matter their age, are sexual, animalistic creatures who, subconsciously or consciously, regard women primarily as partners who can fulfill their basic mating needs. With so many sexual enhancement drugs being advertised, it is obvious that this need or desire is quite important to men.

As I thought this, one of the first profiles I read only confirmed my suspicions. His catchphrase was "Loves To Dance," and part of his profile read:

> Let's be honest here, ladies. I'm looking for an attractive woman who is sexually stimulating. It's all about the electrifying chemistry that begins the dance of lovers. I say this only after years of research and personally acquainting myself with enough women to make Wilt Chamberlain wilt.

Aha! Refreshing! Finally, total honesty. It was amusing but also a complete turnoff, so I moved forward to the next dancer on the page.

Chapter 2

My dance card was empty and ready for its first appointment. My first dance was the modern dance, the contemporary dance of beginners.

The Contemporary Modern Dance: Energy, passion, fluidity in movements and improvisation are some of the cornerstones of this dance form, which is different from classical dances in terms of style and moves. It is its own form of expression. Contemporary dance gives aspiring dancers the opportunity to seek the joy of dancing; it's a dance for beginners, offering partners a chance to get to know one another from a new perspective.

My first dance partner's profile looked charming, and he clearly had a way with writing words for the screen. Ah, but he was only five-eight—which is what I noticed first. Isn't that curious, I thought. I reflected that maybe my interest in height stemmed from memories of towering over middle school boys; perhaps, being large, I never felt feminine even though I wanted to. I knew this was clearly a psychological hang-up, so I have tried to overcome it during my adult life. I kept reading,

despite the potential deal breaker, only because he was adorable. His profile read:

> I know that others will read this but this is
> only written for you, the one person who
> will make my life whole, my life complete.
> My true love. I want you to know how I
> feel about you, what makes me love you the
> way I do.

> You are happy and enjoy living in your
> skin. You appreciate the blessings of life and
> look forward to challenges and adventures,
> however small they may be. You are kind in
> spirit yet strong in your convictions. You
> have a pretty smile that comes from your
> heart and makes your eyes sparkle. When
> you laugh it makes me laugh even more.
> You are a student of the world and enjoy
> different cultures and embrace the diversity
> that makes the world an amazing experi-
> ence. I thank you for being tolerant of oth-
> ers' views that are different from yours. You
> are smart, thoughtful, and understanding.

> You take good care of yourself. You
> look great in your black dress but are just
> as pretty in your favorite jeans and t-shirt.
> I love you when you get up in the morn-
> ing and I give you your first cup of coffee.
> With your sleepy eyes and frumpy hair, I
> pull you close to me and kiss you softly and
> welcome you into another wonderful day
> of our life together. You are a good friend
> and those around you can count on you to
> be there for them. You have opened your

heart and let me in to share your life, your dreams, and even your sorrows.

You love kids, dogs, football (well, maybe hahaha), romantic dinners, quiet walks in the park, hot days at the beach, and cold martinis. We will travel the world together and never tire of our time together. It's our love that makes this adventure the time of our lives. Music is a big part of what we enjoy and we love to dance together. The feeling of the music, the two of us holding each other close just for that moment. We are best friends, we trust each other completely. We are one.

Oh my goodness. What an incredible, thought-provoking read. This is the guy for everyone. Wouldn't it be incredible to have all that was written? A small part of me wondered, is he too short? Maybe that prerequisite should be thrown out the window.

I decided to notify this new dancer with a short message. He in turn replied, and the beginning of communication commenced. The pleasantries were lovely and the e-mails began to flow effortlessly. I could tell this man was well educated, and sure enough, I soon found out that he was an English professor. He wrote:

You have so many wonderful things in your profile and you put so much of yourself into it. I love what you wrote and it is so much more than you see on this site. The depth of your thoughts and feelings says so much about you. You care, I can see that. It's very endearing. Thank you girl.

I read every word more than once, but baby your format was so hard to read. I must admit I had the most fun proofreading and touching up your profile. I cannot tell you how much I felt connected to you as I read your profile; I thought a few changes might help and then all those hunky guys would actually read it. Haha OMG what am I doing?????

I must admit that as I got to the end of your profile, my heart sank: "I'm not searching for a long-term commitment."

Maybe we were not a good match; it was sad but probably true, I thought. At the very least, we could continue talking and comparing notes. But as the weeks passed, there was little more to communicate. It appeared that Mr. Contemporary had dropped from the site, not unexpectedly, possibly to pursue a new dance partner. I discovered later that such was the case when Mr. Contemporary showed up again on the dating site. He wrote then:

I'm back. I turned off my profile because I think it is totally impossible to try to focus on finding out if someone might be the right person for you when these sites throw people at you. Most people who you meet are normal (and I use the term liberally). I was on a second date with a woman who I thought was in the normal range, but it turned out to be the weirdest experience and I literally had to run away as fast as I could. At least at the time it was a bit disturbing. It wasn't Friday the 13th, but it was just a bit like *The Twilight Zone.* Can you hear the music playing? I'll tell you about it sometime.

I promise I won't run away from you. Hopefully some hunky guy hasn't run off with you yet?

Despite Mr. Contemporary's hopeful tone, we never went on a date. Our Internet friendship continued, but never progressed. I was glad that he was the first person I communicated with because he turned out to be a fun and interesting friend, even years later.

Chapter 3

My dance card was beginning to fill, and the next dances were enlightening as well as disappointing. Perhaps that was to be expected; it's a challenge for a couple to produce something beautiful and mutually satisfying together without any firm foundation. Practice was my mantra; the more often I danced and the more partners I danced with, the greater the likelihood of success. Dancers filled the rough cardboard surface of my dance card, a card that might lead me to partnership on and off the dance floor. The question remained, which dance would best suit my style and abilities? Only by dancing with new and varied individuals could I hope to find out.

Mr. Slow presented himself as a normal, kind, and caring man with a wholesome, normal, consistent life. His profile read:

> I like to enjoy life to the fullest. I would describe myself as honest and trustworthy. I think the best of people and look for the best in all situations. I like to stay active and enjoy many things. I have found it is not what you do as much as who you do it with that matters the most.

Wow! This guy sounds like a keeper, I thought. He was a very handsome man in his mid-fifties, much younger looking than his age, and he had been divorced for 19 years. He was ready for retirement and wanted to enjoy life with someone in similar circumstances. I too was at that stage in my life, and needed a partner that could identify with this. A response from me was imminent and thus an e-mail exchange ensued. For a few weeks we exchanged pleasantries and boosted each other's egos. From the outside, it must have looked like we each thought the other was the absolute best thing that ever hit this planet. Mr. Slow wrote:

> You are not only a beautiful lady on the outside but also on the inside. I can see that you truly care about your family and life. We have both been blessed with good family and health.

A revelation and openness ensued. He told me that he had been alone for some time, and that after a lot of soul-searching and reading books on relationships he saw the mistakes that he had made:

> I had the wrong ideas of what was important in life. I worked too much and I learned that you cannot take anyone for granted. You always need to take time every day for that special person in your life. It's the little things that keep a couple together. I am always happiest when I can do something for someone. An acked of kindness only takes a short time but leaves a long impression.

Hm. "An acked of kindness"? Being a stickler for correct grammar and the importance of education, I should have realized that perhaps Mr. Slow was not as well educated as I was. Then again, I thought, I shouldn't critique every little word written. The sentiments were thoughtful, even wonderful; who wouldn't be impressed when men often have a difficult time expressing compliments and sensitivity? Besides, the error could have been a function of the spell check on the computer or something totally benign. I decided to proceed. Oh, and yes, his height did meet my prerequisites.

Mr. Slow was the first man to capture my interest after 30 long and supposedly fulfilled years with another man. What a thrill, all of a sudden, to be able to move in the direction of potential love! I felt like a teenage girl experiencing her first date. It was awesome, scary, and quite confusing, to say the least.

The primary difference between dating now and 30 years past is the maturity that individuals bring to the table—or so I thought. Having experience and wisdom about people and life should have made dating feel less complicated. Unfortunately, being thrown into this new kind of dating after so many years away from dating altogether only created unrealistic expectations. I felt the newness of falling in love again, the excitement of being on the cloud, and dreamed of never ending beds of white roses while the fireworks blazed in my head. When I was supposed to be logically assessing a new partner, and all the intricacies that go along with inviting another person into my life, I had inadvertently reverted back to the kind of infatuation I felt as a teenaged girl. Even when middle-aged people bring intelligence and wisdom to the dance floor, we can still be blindsided by the extreme high of the drug of excitement. In the haze of infatuation, even the best intentions to make decisions with long-term interests in mind can be subordinated to the desire for immediate gratification. No matter how old you are, love is a powerful drug.

My dance with Mr. Slow began quite slowly, though we both believed that ours was the perfect match on and off the dance floor. I decided not to communicate with other men on the dating website while I explored this new relationship with a man who seemed to possess all the qualities that I had listed on my profile page.

Our first meeting was lunch in the middle of winter. The giddiness and childlike feelings that passed over me when the time came to meet my first dance partner are nearly indescribable; that first moment will be etched into my mind for some time. Who was this handsome gentleman who I would be meeting? Should I trust that he is not a deviant? Would I be safe in the company of someone whom I had never met before? Those questions dissipated quickly after I first saw my new dance partner. When he drove up to my car and first glanced my way, a broad and toothy smile with genuine kindness spread across his face. Swiftly, he emerged from his car to open my door, and greeted me, "Hello, so nice to meet you. Would you like to ride with me to the restaurant?"

My first thought was, Oh boy, should I really be getting into this car with someone I just said hello to? Will this be safe? There was no one around to protect me from what could have been a disastrous outcome if he hadn't been all that he appeared to be. Yet something inside me said, it will be okay. Go ahead.

As we approached the restaurant, I worried what we would talk about. I struggled to remember the really important things to discuss when first meeting someone. As it turned out, I needn't have worried. It was a long and interesting conversation at first, but after the initial excitement of meeting wore off, our conversation turned somewhat one-sided as I learned all about my new dance partner and his life. He had a very large family with complicated dynamics, and they all lived in the same city. It wasn't my city; our homes were over 100 miles apart. It seemed not to be a problem at first, but the logistics of our relationship turned out to be a bit difficult, especially for a couple who hoped to practice dancing. But I didn't know that yet, and the date ended with a hug and a hesitant Mr. Slow asking, "Can I call you? I would like to see you again."

I said, "Of course."

Our next date was a dinner date, allowing us more time to get to know one another in a comfortable setting. The scary moments were over, and now we would dance the best way we knew how. This union with Mr. Slow proved to be quite a lovely and joyful one, filled with mutual respect and admiration. In the many weeks and months that followed we went to the theatre, we dined together often, and we met each other's families.

A very conservative dancer, Mr. Slow's ability to react was just that, slow and a bit on the awkward side. It took a lot of practice on the dance floor before he was ready to move to the bedroom. That first time that I was swept off my feet and into a more intimate kind of dance happened on a trip to Chicago in the middle of December. We booked a hotel room and made plans for entertainment and lovely dining as a prelude to a night of romantic ecstasy. This would be my first intimate experience with a new dance partner in 30 long years.

That evening began with loving embraces as we took a carriage ride through the city. It was almost too magical; the snowflakes gently billowed down to the warm earth like a light sheet of crystal gems magically enveloping our bundled-up bodies. The night's chill afforded us a sense of urgency to fall into one another's warm embrace. Huddling close to each other's warm yet shivering bodies, we gazed into each other's aged and weary eyes after a long day of wonder and then moved, ever so slowly, into that first kiss of passion. The kiss was soothing, soft, and sensual; the next kisses were more passionate, and progressed to a more animalistic urgency. We wanted more. After all, here were two individuals who had been deprived of love and sex for a very long time. That night was filled with long passionate kissing that seemed to go on for hours. The thought of being together was at the forefront of our minds. We were both oblivious to those around us, and I'm sure the mass of Christmas revelers in the big city paid no attention to the two of us, either. As the night advanced, we both felt the desire to retire to our hotel. We were anxious to continue this dance slowly and with respect, but we were filled excitement.

As we approached our hotel, the anticipation of what we would experience together, alone in a room of private wonder, increased those feelings of lust and fantasy. Standing at the door of our hotel room, we embraced for what seemed like an eternity. Let's get this dance going, I thought. As two inexperienced dancers, we were both a bit awkward at first. We took off most of our clothes before shyness set in and we wondered exactly how to begin to show our bodies to each other, to explore each other. The sense of having to expose myself to someone new was quite mystical; I felt I was a character from a movie, as if I were watching two completely different individuals playing out the act of intimacy. The disrobing accomplished, our bodies enveloped one another. Our movements were a bit mechanical at first, but true desire was there. Being shy about nudity at our age, we were both eager to hop under the covers.

The night was lovely, but nothing spectacular. The love-making was not forced, but it wasn't what I had expected; it was more of a discovery of sorts. Certainly it was a night that led us to comparisons with our former spouses. To feel comfortable enough with a new partner in discussing what we were really feeling, I felt would only serve to demystify the moment. This was a moment that we all longed for, and most likely idealized, with someone new. Mr. Slow was a man who believed in male dominance in the bedroom; the missionary position was all he knew and all he was prepared to experience that night, perhaps because he lacked a partner for so many years. Maybe his past experiences did not encourage him to experiment with new moves. That night, satisfaction was only for the man. I was not ready to deflate his ego by expressing my dissatisfaction with his moves. It just wouldn't be the polite thing to do. I had been raised, after all, in an era where a woman satisfied the man. His needs exceeded that of a woman's. The night of intimacy ended quickly. We went to sleep was soon after.

The dance continued for the next few months. Sexually, it was as if we were an old married couple; nothing was quite as exciting as I would have expected given the newness of the relationship. There were other challenges, too. One doubt that loomed in my mind was how well I would fit in with a working class family that had little or no education, even though they all had big hearts and souls. Since I had been raised in a differ-ent kind of household, I found it extremely difficult to meld into Mr. Slow's family's lifestyle. Another problem was that our time together was limited to the weekends since distance made it impractical to meet during the week. It was not a conventional relationship, and the months that followed involved many major family events: two weddings, the births of three new grandchildren, a father's death, and a sister's psychotic breakdown. And my new dance partner suffered a tragic injury. During Mr. Slow's recovery, it became apparent that he desperately needed someone to care for him. I became a nurse, psychologist, caretaker, potential stepmother, step-grandmother, and sister-in-law. All these new challenges and roles didn't allow us enough space to develop as couple, and I began to question where the relationship was going. Was this the future that was in store for me?

Despite all the terms of endearment and flowers and dinners and proclamations of eternal love, it was all too good to be true, and too much too soon. I wasn't ready to reciprocate, and I was not prepared for the possibility of a long-term partner in my life so soon after I started dating again. I needed to think it through. The dance seemed to drag on and on; our lack of common ground in conversation and education, as well as other aspects of our lives, led to boredom. The drag of our feet along the dance floor became cumbersome and agonizing. It became all too clear that we had rushed into a relationship. I had been swept off my feet at first, but the fantasyland of newness and wonderment lasted only a short while. When reality set in, I realized we were two completely different individuals who had very little in common.

I realized too late that the logistics of our relationship wouldn't work out, and in time both dancers would fall flat on their faces after a whirlwind of anxiety. The end of the slow dance was painful. For two years, we had seen each other only weekends, with only an occasional trip extending four to five days to break up the routine. Mr. Slow would have been happy to continue with things as they were, but I couldn't endure the boredom of the repetitive, slow, and expressionless moves. After lengthy discussions, we finally mutually agreed to end the dance. Our hands parted and we took our separate paths. Sadly, we never really spoke again.

After much thought and review of what transpired with my first dance partner, I saw a clear picture emerge: I had fallen into full-fledged commitment too soon. Apparently this is a common pattern among newly separated, divorced, or widowed singles—the need to latch onto someone, to feel the sense of permanence and security that comes with being a couple. Today's society is couple oriented, and the fear of being alone is an enormously wasteful emotion, which can lead us too quickly into a new dance with a total stranger. We expect to find great satisfaction from a new union after the abrupt shock of divorce, but that expectation, combined with the newness and excitement involved in finding a new partner, often takes precedence over good judgment and both dance partners move too quickly into an exclusive relationship.

This important realization enabled me to continue the search for a partner who could fulfill a majority of my needs, wants, and desires. I knew that no relationship would be perfect, but that time and careful study would be paramount in developing a more satisfying outcome for both parties.

Perusing all the potential profiles once again seemed a daunting and exhausting task. Still, I started all over again, scrutinizing every little word that was staring at me on the pages of the lost and lovelorn. My dance card had many songs and dances left to fill in.

Chapter 4

I took a break for a month or two after things with the first dance partner ended, and then I started to feel the time was right to look for a man who could stimulate my senses.

I will refer to my next partner as Mr. Tango. It may take two to tango, but in this form the man leads the woman. The tango is danced with the partners in either an open embrace, in which the dancers have space between their bodies, or in a close embrace, in which the lead and the follower connect chest to chest or hip to hip. The steps include small, syncopated, rhythmic footwork, long gliding steps, and complex dance figures. Sometimes the embrace is opened briefly to allow for more complicated footwork. One form of tango uses body dissociation for leading, walking with firm steps, contact, and permanent combinations with an on and off beat or rhythm. The tango is musical and playful.

It was immediately apparent that this new dance partner was the lead; the man took control and it was up to him how and whether this dance would succeed or fail. I was familiar with this type of relationship, although it was not my ideal. I had hopes that I would be wrong, and that Mr. Tango would surprise me with a mutual partnership. The dance began during my daily perusal of five men who fit my requirements. The first image that I noticed was a close-up portrait of a gentle-looking man with a wide smile and sweet eyes hidden by wire rimmed glasses. The picture was especially appealing to me. What turned out to be behind that gentle and sweet appearing demeanor was a surprise to me, especially because I consider myself a good judge of character and, above all, decency. Maybe I was fooled because this well-groomed man in his mid-fifties looked so clean cut. A quick glance at his written profile showed that he was precise, analytical, and organized. Perhaps an engineer, I thought. After numerous photos and accolades regarding his accomplishments, building grand homes and establishments all around the Midwest, I surmised he was a developer. Reading on, his wording was exact and carefully though tout with a hint of religious fervor. Phrases such as "God bless," "God is love," and "faith be with you" suggested that he was a man who may have lost his way at one point and latched onto the intangible for guidance and support.

We e-mailed back and forth, asking all the usual questions about each other's lives, both past and present, and what brought us to this particular site. This tango started out slowly and methodically. Communication was occasional but consistent throughout the next few weeks; the delays between responses lessened the desire for instant gratification. Neither dancer wanted to initiate the next crucial step for fear of stepping on another's toes, or for fear of being the one stepped on; we both knew how much work the dance required. Sometimes I felt rejection, and sometimes I felt that we were playing an unpleasant game. Finally we cleared the air and decided to start over.

With a fresh start, we felt an ease that allowed for free movement, giving each partner the confidence to take that next step: talking on the phone. This step is crucial to deciding whether there might be some hope for a connection, maybe because it adds a sensory component to communication. In this case, I'd already found Mr. Tango's pictures appealing, and hearing this man's voice would tell me about the manner in which he carried himself, and also, quite frankly, what his upbringing may have been. Would that voice be as sweet as the face? Would it be deep, soothing, calm, commanding, chaotic, or comforting? Internet communication can convey a great deal about a person, especially about their looks, but there's no substitute for hearing a voice on the other end of a line

Surprisingly Mr. Tango, who was six-three and 225 pounds, had a sharp, curt, muted-sounding voice. This was not at all what I expected, and it was a disappointment for sure. Still, I kept talking. The initial phone conversation was interesting, to say the least. Setting up a potential date with a new partner after a lengthy life with someone other than the person on the other end of the phone felt a bit awkward and surreal, even though I'd already done so with Mr. Slow. The initial feelings of guilt subsided over time, and accepting the fact that I was now alone and free to pursue someone new began to feel incredibly exciting. As the conversation continued with this potential new dance partner, my first instinct was to be sensitive to the other person. I showed complete and sincere interest in this dancer, inquiring about his life, family, interests, background, life's journey, and what brought him to this place on the dance floor of dating and love. I have found that letting a man talk almost exclusively about himself at first gives him a sense of importance, boosting his self-confidence and ego, which makes him want to escort me onto the dance floor. This was my plan each time I considered a new dance partner, and my success with this method only solidified in my mind my sense of the vast differences between men and women's needs. Many women, including me, are nurturers by nature and often do not feel the need to be bolstered continually in order to feel a sense of self-worth or confidence. Many men, on the other hand, look for continual reassurance from their partners.

After many phone conversations, we decided to finally take that leap together onto the physical dance floor by setting up an initial face-to-face meeting.

We decided to meet for lunch at a restaurant in a small town halfway between our homes. This seemed safer and less threatening than meeting at either one of our personal homes.

The drive was exciting, and the thought of meeting a new person to begin something unknown was thrilling. As I thought over what I would say, I wondered how we would recognize each other. Would he be attractive? Would I be attractive to him? As I turned into the parking lot with my bright white hybrid, I could see in the distance a tall, quite handsome man, well groomed and impeccably dressed. He wore a light pink shirt and khaki pants that made his legs seem to extend for miles. His cleanly coiffed grey hair and lightly trimmed mustache accentuated the dark, steely blue eyes visible beneath the wire-rimmed glasses. He was walking his beautiful, perfectly groomed white retriever, who I came to discover was also perfectly trained. I could see a glimmer of delight on Mr. Tango's face when I caught his eye.

We hugged and the first words out of his mouth were, "I couldn't believe when I saw you first drive up in your white SUV. It's the exact color and make of car I gave to my wife right before we separated." Oh dear! Was that a good thing or did I remind him of his former wife, lover, best friend, and mother of his two children?

To say the lunch was a success would perhaps be an overstatement. It was pleasant enough, but we spent the whole time talking about him and his life. He didn't ask for much information about me, and I didn't offer much. But that was my plan to begin with, and I stuck with my decision. I am curious by nature, and whether or not a person respects others enough to show interest in them tells me a great deal about that individual's character. In this case, I was not sensing much consideration for me; usually men do stop talking about themselves long enough to get to know me better, but not Mr. Tango. His gave me his sob story about the wife who left him unexpectedly, and the man she left him for. Clearly the divorce left a huge hole in his ego and heart that now was filling with anger. I realized that he wasn't ready to move on yet. He once had the perfect wife, the perfect family, and a business that afforded them a lifestyle worthy of kings and queens, but now knew no life other than one of privilege, and he felt he deserved the whole package. He couldn't believe that anyone would leave him, an athlete who once played football for a Division III school and a successful businessman! Perhaps his ex-wife had felt the same lack of consideration that I was feeling on the date.

The lunch ended with a quick good-bye and "nice to meet you," nothing more. Leaving that little village in the middle of a Midwestern town, I felt complete exhaustion and disappointment. I was exhausted because of all the emotional energy I had expended in anticipation of meeting Mr. Wonderful Tango, when I was hoping I could live up to this ideals. I was disappointed not because I felt rejected but because, quite frankly, he was a schmuck, a man with a bigger head than any mother should ever have had to deliver. I was eager to return home, and looked forward to never speaking to him again. Now it was time to look for another dance partner to fill my dance card.

Chapter 5

Returning to many responses that night on the dating site, I felt discouraged. I began to wonder if all I could expect were unfulfilling, exhausting dances with people who weren't right for me. The next profile to catch my eye had the tagline "Looking for Love in All the Cyberspaces." Clever, but as I read on, it wasn't as clever as I first thought. The tagline, although catchy, meant just what it said—someone looking not for love, but more of a physical relationship, in all the wrong places. Wow, what an eye-opener that was. This handsome man in his mid-fifties was looking only for occasional trysts or, shall we say, one night stands, with women who met his physical expectations. Since he was blunt and quite honest about what he wanted, I was able to click "no thanks" and move on to the next profile, all the while wondering if he would be successful in his quest for unattached sexual encounters. Are there people, men and women, out there who only want this in their lives? That kind of search was certainly not on my conservative radar, nor would it ever be, or so I thought at that moment.

The next tagline to catch my eye was
"Let's dance in the rain. I am so glad you
stopped by." The profile was active, and the

photos seemed recent. The man wrote, "I am looking for a beautiful woman to share special moments with, who will seek out new adventures, travel to exotic places, do fun and exciting things and perhaps live the rest of our lives together." Oh my, how wonderful all of that sounded, but the phrase that caught my attention was "beautiful woman." Why was this person so focused on outward beauty that it was a prerequisite? Was he just looking for eye candy to have by his side? Would he be interested in a woman who was beautiful on the inside and not so attractive on the outside? No, probably not. I decided he was shallow and selfish, and I moved on to the next profile suggested from my daily five.

This third profile's tagline was "Lost in hello: seeking a lifelong friend and companion. I try to live a life that God and my kids would be proud of. It hasn't always turned out so good, but that has been my goal. Your all capitals make me dizzy." Criticism! I felt a little stung, since I did write my profile in all capitals at first, never giving much thought to the fact that it was not the best way to write a lengthy profile. In any case, even if a person felt this way, saying so right off the bat was no way to introduce oneself for the first time. It came across as critical, assertive, and uncaring. I scratched this person off the list of my potential dance partners.

The next tagline was "Sensuous adventurous man seeks partner with beauty and grace and depth." Beneath, he wrote, "I can appear complex with a good deal of depth and sensitivity but not too deep down you'll find a playful person willing to laugh and explore." What in the heck did he mean by "depth"? A quick glance at the photos and a little bit of his background revealed a not so good-looking man who felt confident enough to think he deserved the best and would not settle for less. Most men that I read about were very selective in who they dated or would even consider as a partner; this kind of closed-mindedness turned me off. I moved on.

"Looking for the right one, a song sung by a hopeless romantic," proclaimed the next tagline. "Hello ladies," he continued, "what are the chances of meeting you in the grocery store? Probably slim to none. If someone bumps your grocery cart that might be me trying to break the ice." Very cute, I thought; his tagline reminded me of a song by Dan Fogelberg, a favorite of mine. "Met my old lover in the grocery store"—very sad, poignant, and a reminder of loves lost in the past, and also that one cannot go back to a life that was once so familiar. I sent a quick wink and a short message to let this gentleman know that I was impressed with his clever opening statement, and liked his overall profile. He was an adorable man, settled in a professional career and divorced with three children all out of the house. After a few messages with the usual pleasantries, I realized that he was only five-eight—too short. It was shallow, and even hypocritical given how I felt about men who specifically stated they were looking for beautiful women, but I wanted to date a man who was taller than me, and I couldn't let it go. Besides, many men are intimidated by taller, larger women. Within his profile he also stated his desire to date a shorter woman, one of smaller stature. The knowledge that we were both thinking the same made it easy to say good-bye and wish each other luck in our quests to find someone to fulfill all our dreams and desires. I realized that from then on, I should read profiles more carefully before communicating.

The next tagline caught my eye immediately: "The feeling is gone and I want it back." I loved the short and funny introduction that followed: "My 30-minute infomercial: Extra for shipping and handling. Guarantee option available. I am rather tall (6'6")—not overweight, just over tall." What a riot! I thought he might be someone fun to meet. I winked this time. He was online, and after a few moments, I got a response. I am sure he had perused my profile and, of course, scrutinized my photos before replying:

"So you like tall men?"

"Of course, but they have to have substance," I typed back.

A nice conversation via the site ensued. Here was the third dancer to be placed on the card. I called him Mr. Two-Step, because he reminded me of a Country/Western dance. He was a lumbering, massive man in his mid-forties from a state south of mine. His e-mails were pleasant and intellectual, but not overly so. He had never married, but had devoted himself to the educational system for many years. His work toward several PhDs left him little time for a social or romantic life, but in his free time his life was fast paced and high rolling. He liked fast cars, fast cigarette boats, sailing, and horses. When he told me, "I haven't met one person online. Not one," I immediately retorted: "You've met me."

He told me that he was trying to exchange his fast style of living for a more simple, relaxed life. After bringing his trailer of horses to a farm in southern Wisconsin weekly, he traded his big boats and cars for steam tractors and the farm life. How fascinating to hear about people's differing lives! I had to meet him even, if it was for nothing more than an interesting conversation.

We decided to meet up one night when he was in town. It wouldn't be until later in the evening, so we made reservations at a local pub. I wanted to arrive early to check him out as he walked in the place. I knew I couldn't miss him. I hadn't really seen a clear photo of Mr. Two-Step's face, so it would be a total surprise to me, which could be either wonderful or disastrous. In any case, it was a challenge, and one I was ready to meet. As I sat at the front of the pub, I watched people come and go, but half an hour went by with no sign of Mr. Two-Step.

Then there was a brief text followed by a phone message apologizing for his delay. He seemed to have difficulties with his directions, and couldn't locate the place. Forty-five minutes went by, and patient as I was, I began to think I was being stood up. Perhaps he got cold feet; after all, I was his first online date, and he didn't know what to expect or how all it worked. At the instant I was about to leave, I noticed a larger-than-life man with legs up to his elbows, a huge framed body and long, flowing, slicked-back grey locks. There was grimness, but also a sense of nervousness, coming from this dancer, and his footing was unsteady to say the least. Fumbling as he approached the door, no doubt embarrassed about being late, this command-ing gentleman asked me a question.

"Where did you get that smile?"

"Why thank you. My mother, I suppose," I said.

"Don't let it get to your head."

How odd, I thought. He'd given me a compliment and a snide remark all in a moment's conversation. Stroking his long fingers through his windswept and coarse hair, he apologized with fervor for his tardiness.

"Boy, when I saw you sitting there, I thought, I made this beautiful lady sit and wait for me." That made it all better. At least he was a gentleman about it. As I examined this gigantic man in a freshly ironed preppy light-blue shirt, clean, pressed, faded jeans and an expensive, yet visibly worn, pair of saddle-colored cowboy boots, my first thought was, where does he buy his clothes? I have big brothers, but this man was *enormous*. As he maneuvered his long legs and body into the booth, I could see why he might be a bit awkward around women; maybe because of his size he was insecure. However, he seemed to take charge when ordering food, which I thought was charming. Not knowing if I liked alcohol, he politely offered the wine list. I declined, and we both ordered soft drinks.

The rest of the evening was informative but not so fun. As I expected, he was quite an intellectual and possibly a savant who became extremely successful in life financially and socially, but never romantically. This seemed difficult for him, though perhaps he felt detached to some degree out of a fear of possible inadequacy. I will never know because we only met once, and we never communicated again. When he walked me to the parking lot, he asked if he could call again, but that call never came. I left Mr. Two-Step to his life of solitude, as I suspect he wanted. Those cowboy boots would never two-step onto the floor with me.

Chapter 6

That night left doubts in my mind about the honesty of those individuals who claimed they were looking for that perfect dance partner in life. Was this merely a game? I felt as if I were on a never-ending spinning wheel of emotional ups and downs about love and life, personalities, and connections. But I was ready for the next dance on my card.

The profile in front of me was lengthy and complicated to read at best. The picture showed an ethereal yet earthy man in his mid-fifties. I searched for the vital statistics. Marital status? Divorced. Children? Two kids, grown and out of the house. Religious affiliation? None. Height? Six-two (tall). Appearance? Mousey brown hair and glasses that could have been taken from the pages of a discolored yearbook. Here is what he wrote to me:

> I once read that a man falls in love with a woman who he feels attracted to but a woman becomes attracted to a man who she loves. When taken in context women are the ones who retain the power of determining what is to become of any relationship. What a conundrum to now attempt

to circumnavigate to find a best friend with whom to have such a relationship. Physical attraction emanates from a tiny spot deep down where the spinal cord connects to the brainstem, such that upon a sufficient stimulus, the brain is automatically flooded with dopamine. I can now unabashedly and unequivocally state that upon having taken notice of your profile, provided me as a potential match, your physical natural beauty and photogenic presence triggered my brain to become autonomically flooded with dopamine. Yup my old brainstem determined after an exceedingly fleeting moment with my optic nerves and retinal tissues that you're damned hot and I too should be added to the usual list of what in all likelihood is the entirety of mankind that has similarly found you to have been so extremely attractive, as was my impression. With that having been so fully established, I thereafter also found myself to have thoroughly enjoyed having read the rest of what was shared in your profile's provided content. The conscious halves of the rest of my brain having become equally impressed as had my brainstem, I came to the belief that we might share much in common, so much as to have triggered my wonderment regarding if you might find any reciprocal interest to be taken in me. I would surely enjoy taking on any opportunity to learn more about you and taking at least another baby step walking further forward in this discovery process. I sincerely thank you for having made me smile to know that a woman in your caliber might yet still

remain to be discovered on any site like the
one I have been to so search for sentiment
in life discovered here.

This guy cannot be serious, I thought, as I continued to read on and on and on. Maybe this was a joke. Maybe it wasn't a joke and this guy was from another planet. Maybe techno dance would suit him. He seemed robotic and calculating, and, to me, emotionless. I wondered, if this man writes and thinks in this calculating and long-winded way, how would anyone carry on a meaningful and understanding conversation with him without getting lost in the garbled mumbo jumbo and phonetic rhetoric of confusion? How could things proceed to intimacy? How could anyone be in the moment with him calculating and talking without things ending in disaster? I couldn't consider this dancer for my card.

As I clicked over to the next profile, a surprising message appeared. It was a kind and sweet greeting from Mr. Tango: "I would love to make you dinner at my lake home."

His invitation for a second round of discovery was tempting. First impressions are important, but sometimes people are so ill at ease about that first meeting that they can't relax and be themselves. I thought I should allow for this, even given Mr. Tango's previous self-centered behavior, and so I accepted his invitation with enthusiasm and grace. I wrote back, "I would love to see you again. You sound like such an interesting man with so much to tell. I need to hear more."

My approach was gushy, and naturally Mr. Tango was delighted. We agreed to see which dates worked best for both of us. It was summer, and the days and evenings were long, so spending time at a cabin overlooking a lake was extremely attractive to me. We picked a date, but before we could meet, I received a surprise phone call from Mr. Tango.

"Hi, I'm sorry to say that I don't think I will be able to have you visit. A conflict has arisen—I will be judging a beauty pageant that weekend and will be indisposed. Maybe we can do it another time?"

I sighed inwardly. He was too busy; he was very important in his small community and made every effort to let me know it. I thought to myself, *no problem*. He's big fish in a small pond; let him wallow in his glory while he misses out on all that I have to offer. Was his phone call supposed to impress me? I wasn't impressed, just a bit disappointed, but only because I had discovered that as I became more involved with one individual, the anticipatory excitement outweighed all the possible conflicts. I settled down to wait. The waiting was long, but after a three-week hiatus I heard from Mr. Tango again. He was going to be in my area, driving through on a work-related business trip during the day, so he could take me to dinner on my turf. I agreed.

We decided to meeting at restaurant of my choice since I knew the area. I declined his offer to pick me up at my home for security reasons, and because I wanted to avoid certain impressions; it takes time to get to know a person. I chose a lovely steak place in the heart of the city. On a warm and balmy summer evening, I decided to put on the ritz, since it was clear that this dance partner enjoyed a show. Slipping into one of my more tight-fitting and elegant black sleeveless dresses, I decided to forgo underwear and nylons. With my favorite complementary stiletto pumps to finish the look, I knew I would impress him. I felt elegant and classy, yet comfortable. I did my hair and makeup, but skipped jewelry because I figured simple was better, and many times less is more. That is who I am, and I wouldn't compromise that for anyone.

Meeting at the restaurant, I was greeted by the large-framed and handsome Mr. Tango. He immediately took my hand and guided me through the door as if to declare that he was in control, and that I should once again follow his lead. Sitting at the elegant and dimly lit bar, we engaged in a casual yet very comfortable exchange of information, mostly centered on him again. As I scanned the dining area to see if there might be anyone I knew, I was alarmed to see several couples who I considered friends from my past life. I felt a whole new kind of insecurity. I felt nervous about being seen with someone other than my ex-partner. It was uncomfortable because the dynamics had changed; I was no longer the wife of the familiar partner. I could be regarded as the enemy of sorts, I thought. Loyalties were divided between our once mutual friends and acquaintances. Aside from my personal circle of friends, I was the one who was left out of the once-familiar couple's group, the untouchable, the leper in my new life.

I decided then that it didn't matter; I understood the dilemma and faulted no one. I determined the best approach to this situation would be to go out of my way to greet them. I would pave the way for a more comfortable environment and eliminate what could have been an extremely awkward situation. Approaching the couples with confidence and open arms, I was rewarded with a hug and a huge sigh of relief. A good move, I thought, and certainly the tensions in the air had cleared. I turned to a woman I'd known for years, but hadn't spoken to in a long time.

"Hello, it's been so long. How are you?" I said.

"So wonderful to see you. How have you been, and the girls?" she said.

"I am well, and so are the girls. I would love for you to meet my friend."

All eyes peered up at this gloriously handsome and commanding man with approval. I am sure they were very curious about the man I was dating, and I guessed at their eagerness to tell their other friends and my ex about him. Though the anxiety regarding being seen with someone else would continue for awhile, overcoming it became easier and easier as time went on. I was so glad to have cleared this first hurdle.

After we moved to our own table, the dinner was long, and the conversation again revolved around my partner. I heard all about his life and all that he achieved from a very young age to the present. Once more he suggested that I should feel sorry for him because he was jilted by a wife who he thought adored and admired him. Though Mr. Tango's self-admiration was evident throughout the evening, I kept to my plan: I would allow my partner to take the reins and see if there would be any opening for me to enter into this one-sided dialogue.

The elasticity of the tango's open embrace should have allowed for Mr. Tango to lead the conversation in many directions, but he kept dancing on the same patch of floor. With great patience, I allowed the self-absorbed conversation to continue. It was during dessert that I thought to myself that if I was going to continue dancing with him, the time had come that I should at least impart some information of my own. In a firm tone I asked, "Is there something you would like to ask me about my life?"

Yikes, that was a shock! Mr. Tango stopped dead in his tracks, looked at me sternly with those steely blue eyes *now* visible through the wire-rimmed glasses and replied, "My, you're blunt. You don't mess around, do you? I am not sure I have any questions for you."

"Okay then," I responded, "I will tell you a little about myself." He was trapped for the time being so he had to listen, or at least pretend to listen. I continued, "I was married for a long time, and I have two beautiful, accomplished daughters. The dissolution of my marriage was devastating at the time, but I have come to accept all that has happened in my life. I've been excited to discover talents and interests that I never thought would surface. It's been enlightening and extremely positive."

At this very moment, I felt the need to impress this man with a list of my accomplishments and accolades. I began, "I've earned several degrees in very different areas of study. I taught at the college level and then went on to become a registered nurse working in a hospital setting, in clinics, and in public health. After retirement, I began pursuing my talents as an artist. Having oil paintings exhibited in prominent art galleries in New York City, I was also on consignment with many businesses for their offices. I worked under the famed Leonard Baskin, a contemporary printmaker. I have written and illustrated children's books and am currently commissioned to illustrate several Californian poets' books. I love the theatre and singing and I appeared in many theatrical productions along with well-known Hollywood actors. Modeling for television and catalogues has afforded me many luxuries. And I come from a large, very accomplished family." But I decided to put all my accomplishments aside in favor of impressing Mr. Tango in an arena I knew he cherished. Here came the crème de la crème.

"My brother was a professional athlete, a bonus baby in Major League Baseball. He signed with Gene Autry's California Angels and went on to play with other Major League Baseball teams. He was a poster boy on the Wheaties box and courted many Hollywood starlets. That time in our lives was incredible, being hosted by major professional teams in football and base-ball. We appeared in magazines like *Sports Illustrated* and *Life*. It provided an interesting life for the whole family."

Elaborating was not necessary. At this point, I had slapped Mr. Tango in the face with a little one-upmanship. He never saw it coming. Shazam! I felt wonderful.

Still, I knew that things weren't going to work out between us, so I led the conversation back to him, where I knew he'd be comfortable: "Um, did you say you played in a Division I col-lege team, or was that Division III?" This dance was over, not soon enough for me. Curiosity kept me at the table—curiosity to see just how long one person could expound upon himself. As he talked, I realized that he needed a Barbie doll, a beauty queen, someone who would look good on his arm and be con-tent to keep quiet while allowing him to be the king. After a quick good-bye and "best of luck to you," we parted ways. The tango was crossed off my dance card for good.

Chapter 7

I felt weary and lovelorn. Searching for that perfect partner seemed like a daunting task, but I wasn't content with the few unfulfilled dances so far. The quest continued.

Weeks went by and the search seemed endless. Each day, many new faces appeared, seeming to beg for the chance to put on those dance shoes and take a trial spin. I was surprised by the variety of men on the site—male models, judges, physicians, nurses, corporate executives, insurance agents, sailors, bikers, pilots, artists, writers, educators, mortgage and real estate brokers, dentists, farmers, iron workers, venture capitalists, and even a concert cellist. I communicated with so many dancers, though, that reading profiles started to feel like a job. I felt obligated to at least politely comment back to those who took the time to stop by to say hi or wink each day.

This was not much fun day after day, but there was always that one profile that popped up to spark my curiosity. For example:

> JAMES BOND FACE, ADAM SANDLER BODY: Original personality, sugar bear voice, gifted and blessed, warm and witty. Let's talk. I want a lot. And I offer more. Have

enough money for the rest of my life, as long as I am dead by Thanksgiving. Love writing headlines and short stories. Perform improv and record. Ideal woman is not expected. THERE IS NO PERFECT 10. TOO MANY VARIABLES MAKE A PERFECT SCORE BEYOND REALITY. I AM NOT A 10. On a good day I might approach an 8.2 with no East German or Soviet judge holdovers. A nun asked me in eighth grade, "WHAT MAKES YOU THINK YOU ARE SUCH A PRIZE?" That was in response to getting my dance card tweaked for the eighth grade dance. That taught me a life-long lesson.

Cute, I thought, so a wink was in order. The curt response: "Chicken soup warmth makes me think you are a warm person. But your profile—those capital letters are blinding! You need help rewriting this." I responded, "I will acknowledge your writing expertise, but in the future, never respond with such a negative tone to someone you who approaches you." I think that sent a message that I was not too pleased with the criticism. Maybe once again I could help someone to present himself more positively. He retorted:

My apologies and my pleasure. My advice to edit your profile was arrogant. Write for yourself. I blame the massive germ invasion in my body at the time. I am over that virus now, which was probably from the germ labs of the CIA or CDC. It must have been weaponized.

That was strange enough for me to move on. I had not set foot on the dance floor for some time, and my feet were aching to move. A new batch of profiles came rolling in:

The thirty-eight-year-old single grad student who played guitar for a living.

The man who had been married twice and whose gorgeous wife, a former model who was 15 years his junior, left him for a younger, more appropriately aged man. Our conversations revolved around her and all the lavish gifts and trips he afforded her, only to be left alone. He clearly hadn't moved on.

The extroverted entrepreneur who posted a picture of a very handsome young Joe Namath lookalike but who, when I met him, looked 20 years older, with horribly yellowed or missing teeth. He bore absolutely no resemblance to Joe.

The never-married, insecure man who had a cleft lip and who couldn't get past hello.

The young and successful dancer who was diagnosed with cancer and given only a short while to live. One who I pursued but would never receive responses from. I feared he had succumbed to his life threatening illness. I was still wondering.

The firefighter who was also a smoke-eater and cigar aficionado.

The extremely handsome gentleman who expounded on romance, flirting, seduction, passion, kissing, chemistry, commitments, intimacy, communication, foreplay, soul mates, integrity, and playmates, who never gave me the time of day even after my many attempts to get his attention. It was a good lesson in personalities and how different our expectations are when we look at one another.

Then there was the burly bodybuilder who was obsessed with physical appearance, mostly his own. We met once after two weeks of phone conversations. It was a meeting that will leave me rolling on the dance floor with laughter until the day I die. The first thing he said to me was, "Oh hello! My, you have nice shoulders."

Oh my goodness. Not "My you have lovely eyes" or "You look pretty" or "Nice to meet you. You look lovely today." No. It was, "My, you have nice shoulders; they are very proportionate to your body." I had to take a closer look later that evening, and I had to admit I do have nice shoulders. The Joe Namath quasi-lookalike also made a similar reference, which I still to this day find hilarious.

(I would be remiss if I didn't mention the many *women* who approached me on the dance floor. This was a surprise to me, but a flattering one.)

Along came the next entry on my dance card. Funny how you see a picture and read a snippet of what that person is about, and it may or may not draw you in. This one drew me in immediately. He was ten years younger than I, and his interests and looks were undeniably appealing. An instant chemical attraction I couldn't deny seemed to appear over these waves of streamed telecommunication. I returned to the picture and reread, "Squeeze every drop out of life." In his profile, he wrote about starting a new chapter, and how he wasn't willing to settle. There it was again, not settling for settling's sake. Not limiting himself to exploring just his backyard, he wanted to see what else was out there in the world. He was an elite athlete training for marathons, triathlons, and ironman competitions. Extreme competitions were a big part of his life, but he wrote that he understood the need for a healthy balance and enjoying all the other things that life has to offer. Back to the dance floor I went.

"Hello. Loved your picture profile," I typed.

> "You are lovely. I was reading your profile and thought to myself, *perfect.* Tell me more about yourself," he immediately responded.

Finally someone had the courtesy enough to inquire about my life. So the dance with Mr. Rumba began.

The rumba is the dance of love. The ballroom rumba is the slowest of all the Latin ballroom dances. Steps are compact, with few rising or falling actions. Hips sway over a motionless leg, arms are free to move in various figures. It is sultry, sexy, and tight. Mr. Rumba, with his slow and precise movements, would turn out to be a brilliant dancer. The electrifying musicality of the words we said to one another created an emotional framework for our two bodies that evoked this dance form.

The flow of conversation moved in a positive direction. We both sensed a complete and undeniable attraction, even in cyberspace. There was an air of mystery about Mr. Rumba. He was clearly well educated, and spent a fair portion of his time traveling for business. Both animal lovers, we bonded over our pets. Mine was a new puppy and his an aging, not-so-healthy lab. It was refreshing to compare notes on the love of animals and on their importance in our lives. Watching the Westminster dog show and discussing various breeds over the telephone was so much fun. He would prove to be a wonderful dance on this woman's card.

We decided to meet to see if our online connection would carry over into real life. The first date involved a long distance drive on Mr. Rumba's part. He drove four hours in the middle of winter to meet me for dinner at a local Italian restaurant.

Walking into the dimly lit restaurant with its garishly appointed Italian décor, I saw a charming man with tight, coarse grey hair sitting alone in a small and quite intimate booth. Clearly he took very good care of his body, which he presented in a white polo shirt and light blue jeans. Wearing a fur lined leather jacket, he was a picture of manly delight.

Having already established a connection through e-mails and talking on the phone, we were now ready to examine one another on a real level, to interact without the ability to shut down the conversation by folding our laptops or switching off our tablets at any given moment. There was no escaping now.

"Hi, I'm Annie. So very good to finally meet. You're more handsome in person than in all of those pictures."

His smile was broader than ever, and very welcoming. Now it was his turn.

"Oh my what an introduction, Annie14Bunny. You are stunning!"

As we glanced at one another with approval, I knew we were going to have a lovely evening together. Between the mysterious smiles and obvious delight from both parties, conversation flowed about our lives and interests in the present. Not so much was asked or offered about our pasts. This new partner was looking forward to new adventures, never looking back with regret on the old.

He was so handsome. I hoped that I could continue to spark an interest in him as well. I brought up the age difference, but without hesitation, Mr. Rumba said he never even considered it a factor. Heeven reiterated that I was the most beautiful woman whom he had met on the site. Flattery, flattery, flattery. I couldn't get enough of it. This was a long overdue need for me, after being so shut down and stifled for many years in a long and mundane life with someone who became, to me, only a roommate. Being pumped up once again after feeling deflated by the divorce and my first few dating experiences felt so glorious.

The night ended with an after-dinner cosmopolitan at a local piano bar and a brisk walk through the cold dampness of the winter night. After walking to the parking garage together, we hugged. I said, "Let me know when you are driving through my town again; it would be nice to see each other again." I watched as he walked to his parking space, trying to get a glimpse of the car he was driving, just out of curiosity. It was a Jeep Cherokee with a mounted ski and bicycle rack. Yes, here was a man who was active as his profile said. I wondered if I could live up to this athlete's extreme endeavors. I would soon discover that priorities can become obsessions.

Because the distance between us was so great, we knew it would be unlikely that we could connect physically on a regular basis. That didn't deter either of us from trying to create those dance moves electronically. As the conversations continued, we felt more and more comfortable with each other, speaking freely and sometimes even sexually. This created a stimulating environment for two people starving for the intimate moments we all deserve. And then came a text from Mr. Rumba:

> I think my thoughts of you as one of
> the most beautiful women I have ever met
> have probably clouded my sense of what
> is realistic. I know that I have said that
> distance shouldn't be insurmountable,

but I have to admit that if two people are truly going to get to know each other and take it to the next level, it requires frequent interaction, and hopefully mostly in person. I truly do not want to waste your time although I would still like to continue to get to know you, and visit one another.

Oh dear, I thought. What does this mystery man really want from me so soon? Is he misinterpreting what my motives, needs, and wants are? I replied:

Good morning. First of all, thank you so much for the more than flattering compliments. It is also nice to know how you are feeling about the potential for us to move forward. You do seem to have a little guard up and I find that your written communication allows you more security in expressing yourself, without the fear of my face to face response. I must say you are difficult to read. Honestly I am not sure what I expect from a relationship right now, but as I indicated I am open to any possibilities. When I went to hug you goodbye I felt that I was doing most of the initiating and did not sense much interest from you in return. That is where my confusion set in. As President Reagan said, "Mr. Gorbachev, tear down this wall!" Haha. Let me in. A kiss would have been a wonderful surprise. Whew, cleared the air. I do hope to see you again.

A few days later, a response via the all-too-easy and safe e-mail came:

A couple of things struck me as we were talking at the restaurant. You seemed to make a pretty strong statement that you were not interested in any kind of serious relationship. My reaction to that was that I needed to watch I say about any feelings I may have about you...sort of put up a little barrier maybe. And then when we were out in the parking lot you said something like "let me know the next time you are in town" but I was going to say something more along the lines of "Would you like to see each other again." But when you made your comment, I immediately abandoned my original line of thinking. I'll be totally honest with you and say that I wanted to give you a kiss as we were departing, but it just didn't seem like the right thing to do at the moment. I guess what I am trying to say is that I have been fairly conservative in what I have said to you because I didn't want to be too overbearing, but the fact is I think you are incredibly beautiful and I enjoy every minute talking to you. I don't know how I can make it more clear but our age difference means nothing to me. You look and act 20–30 years younger and I find that unbelievably attractive. Sorry to be blunt. I cannot deny that the distance factor is a little more tricky, but I don't see it as an insurmountable barrier that would prevent us from seeing each other on a more regular basis. That is where I don't know where the "line" is as far as what type of a relationship you are willing to entertain. Am I making any sense? And as far as connections go, for me there is a

very strong connection. Maybe I am just
not good at showing it or maybe just being
a little overly cautious as to not scare you
off. So remind me why you live so far away
from me?

Our texts and e-mails and phone calls became numerous. Checking our calendars (mine was not so busy), we agreed to meet again when he was en route to a marathon in a state south of me. I was so excited to see Mr. Rumba again. I felt like a schoolgirl waiting for her first dance with the boy who made her heart flutter. Interesting, really, how two people who have only met once can create such a bond over long distance communication. I felt I had reached a safe haven, now that I realized that the person I had revealed so much personal information with would be sitting by my side. The question was, had we gotten comfortable enough to take a leap off the dance floor and into the bedroom? In my mind, I was ready to move along with class and grace and allow nature to take its course.

The day arrived, and we were to meet for dinner. I chose casual and comfortable attire for its fluidity and ease. As Mr. Rumba emerged from his Jeep Cherokee, I felt as though someone else had control over my actions. I was that teenage girl, flirtatious and sensual, allowing my love interest to lead me to another form of dance. The bar was empty, and we were in lust with one another. We ordered a pale ale and a white chardonnay to bring down those barriers spoken of earlier. We let our guards down for the evening, and the doors were open for a whirlwind of sexual fantasy. After another glass of wine and a light dinner only, our stomachs were satiated. We needed dessert, and that was waiting at my house.

Entering my safe haven, the home I had made mine after my divorce, I felt a little odd knowing someone else would be admitted into a home I had designed for myself. It didn't take long, though, before we found ourselves immersed in one another's arms. I fell quickly. His passionate and forceful kisses were erotic enough to break down those last remaining walls of apprehension. We caressed each other's bodies, examining the newness of an unfamiliar partner. He was solid, toned, and athletic. Not a big-framed man, but one who had worked his legs in all those endeavors. Muscles upon muscles bulged from the tight-fitting pants he so eagerly slipped down below his ankles. As he rushed to untie his shoes, I began to slowly slip my fingers around the waist of his boxer shorts to ease them over his strong and muscular buttocks, arousing what may have been in slumber for many months. Mr. Rumba had a robust and healthily erect penis, cleanly shaved, with smooth and shiny testicles. *Oh my*, I thought, *he has less hair than I do on my body*. In my day, the waxing and the shaving and the treatment for woman's bodies were never a priority. The natural was the only option. Maybe I needed to rethink the whole Brazilian waxing thing after this. I just hoped he wasn't turned off. Not a chance. He had already gone into the bedroom.

We caressed and stroked one another, savoring every moment. As uncomfortable as I thought I would be with my choices, I preceded to act in my not-so-typical style. I pushed him to the floor, straddling him. I pulled him close to me and inserted the very engorged instrument into my all-too-ready vagina. Looking up at me in amazement, he reached up to caress my face, repeating how lovely I was. He wasn't ready to be gentle, though—he rolled me over and lifted my hips into a kneeling position; he wanted to enter me from behind, giving him the power to control our movements. This would be the first time I had ever experienced such a position. It was a heart-pounding and sexually stimulating feeling. He was not done yet; he had a lot of ideas swirling in his sexually driven mind. Now it was my turn for complete arousal and pleasure. Mr. Rumba was certainly aware that his partner wanted, and needed, to feel as much pleasure as he had. With two hands on my knees, he spread my long legs to an open V, performing those intricate yoga stretches all the while stroking my abdomen and moving his lips toward uncharted territory. It had been years since I felt such arousal. Not even Mr. Slow was capable of producing such an emotional reaction. As Mr.

Rumba slowly kissed and caressed me, warmth and moisture flooded me. I moaned with joy and satisfaction, free to express that long-awaited orgasm. There was a wonderful chemistry between me and this dance partner; we experienced a refreshing union that we rehearsed over and over again. Perfection.

The perfection of this new dancer allowed me to appreciate and adore him as one who took pride in life, work, and love. This rumba would continue on a scale of massive proportions, albeit mostly long distance. As it turned out, all the anticipation generated by the physical distance between us made it more exciting when we could actually connect on a physical level. During the down times, the weeks when we could not see one another, we kept the fantasy of what we had to look forward to going. Never in my wildest imagination had I dreamed that I would enjoy sexual stimulation through the written word, or as most would refer to it, sexting. It was quite erotic, stimulating two people who did know each other on an intimate level in order to keep our arousal flowing. What a rush.

Quick texts during the day aroused the senses and prompted immediate, eager responses. Soon we needed to see one another, and we took the next logical step. An afternoon prompt from my cellular phone notified me that someone had left me a message. Ah, it was Mr. Rumba. With a swift tap of my index finger, out popped for my viewing pleasure a picture of a naked man with a huge smile, exhibiting an enormously erect penis. This was a first. Oh boy, what does a sixty-something conservative woman from a family with strict moral upbringing think about this? Or what does she do about this? He was clearly a sexual human being, maybe hyper sexual, possibly due to his extreme athletic training and his diet of enhancement supplements. I didn't know, nor did I care. He was providing me with much needed mental and physiological endorphins that were very pleasurable. After the shock wore off, the thought of having this dance partner here with me *now,* even in this way, made it apparent that just the sight of him could stimulate me. His gamble worked, and the sexual dialogue continued off and on for the rest of the afternoon. He prompted me with, "What are you wearing now? Would you be comfortable showing me what you look like?"

Okay, I thought, a *polite* request, so with a little trepidation and very little thought of the consequences, I disrobed and revealed my breasts. "Perfect," he said. He told me he wanted to be there with me and caress every inch of my body. I thought, was this cheap sex? Maybe, but I didn't care. I would continue until we were both immersed in the moment. After the thrill died off, and the emotional and sexual fantasies were put aside until the next encounter, I couldn't help but wonder what a man who had reached such an aroused state did to satisfy his need. Immediately, the answer was apparent, and just imagining this man stroking himself to achieve such pleasure aroused me enough for both of us.

Texting or sexting was emotionally and sexually stimulating without the commitment of a relationship. There was a certain kind of safety in the interplay of those written words, even though we both felt increasing vulnerability. Sexual tension began to build as we carefully chose words and phrases, or steps if you will, calculated not to hasten the dance to the end, but to flatter, increasing the interest and excitement of the other partner. All the while I understood that this wasn't the most appropriate kind behavior for developing a normal, healthy relationship. But this dance with Mr. Rumba carried on. Was I curious? As I analyzed my behavior, I realized I was feeling a sense of power. I was an older woman whose self-restraint was slowly disappearing with each release of endorphins. The new sense of control and freedom of action eliminated the fear of reaction or repercussions from judgmental individuals. I was this new dance partner's vessel of desire, and I enjoyed sensually reeling him in during this season of mating, slow and deliberate. The animal need to procreate never leaves us, no matter the age. I am woman, hear me roar.

Mr. Rumba was a perfect partner for now, one who provided me with all the basic needs of a relationship from afar, allowing for the independence and time alone that I was still cherishing in my new life. This dance needed a lot of practice and the end wouldn't happen for a very long time. We would continue to perfect our moves alone and together. As was discovered, the connection would always be there, but the frequency of communication would diminish. We had gradually changed to an occasional "Thinking of you," "How have you been?" or "Will you be driving through my area at any time?" The distance did prove to be an issue, and as I later discovered, my rumba partner eventually ventured into new territories of love with someone who provided that physical connection on a more permanent basis. I had to concede to the new partner, which was a loss for me for sure, but a realistic decision for both of us.

Chapter 8

I hesitated over looking for another dance partner. It was surely a daunting task, but should it feel like a task at all? I asked myself. Maybe finding love shouldn't be this much work; if the match is meant to be, then the moves should flow. The pressure to keep up my appearance as a youthful and sought-after dance partner made me feel anxiety, and it felt unfair. Men are so visual, their egos so fragile, and their expectations are so unreasonable with regard to the importance of dating an attractive woman. Their sense of entitlement only sets them up for continual disappointment. Quite amusing, really, since the numbers of not-so-attractive men were far greater than the numbers of not-so-attractive women on the site.

I received a message that confirmed my thinking. The man wrote, "I'll have to say you are still the best-looking woman on this site. I think we should meet so that I can be sure you are as pretty as your picture." Now how's that for pressure? My insecurities set in at that moment, and then anger followed. Who did he think he was? Why should the woman have to prove to anyone that she lives up to someone's unrealistic ideals? The female sex seems to be a great deal more accepting of human beings' differences, and a great deal more willing to look deeper into the individual and not rely only on surface impressions. As frustrating as this fact was to me, I persisted and continued my search.

The following are a vignettes of meetings I had with dancers—none of whom would be included on this dance card—that would only serve to enlighten me and lead me to pursue other more suitable partners.

Mr. Grind presented himself as a man of extreme confidence and few inhibitions, ready to straddle his partner. The grind sounds more painful than seductive, and it was with this partner.

After few unsatisfying e-mails back and forth, we decided to meet for a quick drink. I decided to do so, even though our communication was horrendous, because I just had to see for myself if this guy was for real. Once again wanting to make a good impression, I agonized over what to wear. It was midsummer, so I had a deep and golden tan going, which lent itself to a sleeveless outfit to accentuate those incredible shoulders I was told I had. I decided on my little black casual sleeveless dress. It was form-fitting and sharp and a bit above the knee, and I paired it with some cute strappy black sandals. I arrived 10 minutes early, ordering a tall glass of sparkling water, sipping slowly so as not to have to rush to the bathroom and miss Mr. Grind's entrance. He arrived 10 minutes late. This stocky and short man wearing a bright pink golf shirt, multicolored plaid shorts, and boat shoes barreled through the door of the restaurant. Looking around at the bar, he thought he spotted me across the room and proceeded to introduce himself to a lovely thirty-something, unattended young woman across the bar. I hurriedly jumped to my feet and interrupted his move.

"Mr. Grind?" I asked.

"Yes?" he replied.

"Hello, I am Annie." Same old line said over and over again. "So nice to meet you finally after all our e-mails." I felt the air of disappointment in his manner at that moment. I think he was hoping for the young woman across the bar. Too bad he was stuck with me for the moment. What arrogance, I thought to myself. Here was a professional man in the dental field with big white porcelain teeth (obviously fake), a broad face with freckly, light-colored burned skin, and a voice that sounded like Kermit the Frog. We sat in the comfy leather chairs to begin the dance. He ordered a drink, and never asked if I might like something else, perhaps an hors d'oeuvre—after all, it was dinner time and he was late because of a golf game that went long into the nineteenth hole with his buddies. He made it clear he was here because he was doing me a favor. He was not impressed, nor was he interested in me as dance partner. Still, I was curious to hear about him.

"Tell me your story. How did you get to the point in your life to find yourself looking for love the on Internet?" I asked.

"After 25 years of a somewhat happy marriage with a woman whom I worked side by side with, I decided I didn't want to be married anymore, and I told her I didn't love her and wanted someone more stimulating."

"Oh, I am so sorry." Egads! First I felt sorry for his wife, but then I thought, gosh, he probably did her a big favor! Here was a narcissistic man with little regard for others, and now she's free of him.

"She got heavy and unattractive, and I just didn't find her appealing anymore. I have two sons, and they are just fine with it all," he continued.

Yeah right, I thought. Those boys are going to have the same ridiculous expectations when they try to find their dance partners. We are all products of our environment and they'd grown up with this egocentric, pompous individual for a father. I listened to him talk, as I usually did with the others. Finally, he inquired about my reason for being in the situation that I was. I was honest and said that I was the woman who was left cruelly, like the way he left his wife.

"It was very painful and difficult at first, but one begins to accept life as it is given to them. I have a wonderful family, and we are all healthy. That is the important thing."

He disrespectfully interrupted, "Oh, I see, he took that knife and shoved it into your back and twisted and twisted it until you were left a core of yourself. Well, I can see we have little in common."

In disbelief, I looked at him and thought, is he joking? No, he wasn't. He knew that by being the initiator of the same scenario, he had little empathy for the other side. I did not want to let this guy get the upper hand of me and so I said, "You know, he was right, and it was the best thing that ever happened to me. I was released from the anxieties and constraints put on me by those that were arrogant and selfish, only to find so many other women like myself finally free from the cancer that could have killed us. See ya." I walked to the bathroom, as I had finished that tall glass of seltzer water, and when I returned, I noticed the bill at my seat. He had left without paying. It was a confirmation of his lack of character.

> The next profile that caught my eye delivered just what it promised: Something out of the ordinary: 52 year old man, 6 ft. 6, divorced with one son, looking to find someone to do things with. Own my own business, performed around the world...I don't have a lot of free time but love to have someone to go to movies, sporting events, concerts, plays, and travel with.

I received a quick wink from this man and I wrote back, "Thank you for the notice. What kind of performing have you done? I am particularly interested because I too love the theatre and music and song and dance." A very modest response from this lovely man was, "Oh, I played the cello." I wanted to know more. I asked him how he had started playing the cello. He wrote back:

> I loved picking up all types of stringed instruments as a child and preferred the larger cello because I am such a big man. I guess I was sort of musically gifted.

Played in symphony orchestras around the U.S. and later had appointments in Japan, Scotland, and Singapore with the Philadelphia Symphony and the New York Symphony Orchestras. Now I make cellos.

Wow, what a fabulous story from an unlikely person. I was hooked. I admired artists in all disciplines so much because I knew how much talent and hard work was involved in all areas of the arts. I needed to know more. He chose to settle in a small university town in the Midwest, which coincidentally was the same town where my daughter was going to college. This would be great. I could visit her and maybe start up a friendship with this most interesting man. That we did. Many e-mails and the exchange of phone numbers began the next chapter in my search for a new dance partner.

I called him Mr. Salsa. A resident of the Latin community, Mr. Salsa was of mixed race. He was a gentle giant with a soulful voice—a tender, generous, adorable teddy bear. He had dark features and lovely warm-toned skin, deep set dark chestnut eyes, and a furrowed brow. His long and gloriously thick black hair was combed sleekly back into cascading waves of voluminous splendor.

Salsa originates from the Cuban song. Dancers move to the beat of many instruments, particularly the congas, timbales, piano, guitar, maracas, and claves. Our dance began by changing the weight of each step, not letting the upper body be affected by the weight change. As our hips moved, we began to incorporate the arms and shoulders, creating a significant rhythm and movement from the waist up. Mr. Salsa became the lead dancer. His communication was open to my eagerness to follow. As our communication became more fluid, much like the flow of this dance, we felt free to incorporate additional body movements, spins, shoulder shimmies, legwork, acrobatics, and lifts. Mr. Salsa was sexy and smooth at improvisation.

His timing, foot patterns, body rolls and movement, turns, and attitude influenced me to respond in a similar manner.

Our first meeting was just that easy. I felt a moment of, *I know you from somewhere. Have we met before?* A mutual feeling warmed over the initial awkwardness I anticipated when first meeting someone. It was as if I were dancing with someone I had known all my life. I felt a real sense of familiarity and connectedness. Could he have been a long-lost relative I didn't know about? Maybe someone I knew in a previous life? Oh, brother, who would believe that? Whatever the eventual outcome with Mr. Salsa, we both knew that we would carry with us a friendship for a very long time.

We spoke only a few words when we met, and then a silence ensued. It was all too easy. Gazing into each other's eyes for the first time, we examined familiar features. "I know you and I am comfortable being with you," we said without speaking. This strange feeling continued throughout our first encounter. The ease of each movement and moment prepared us for an inevitable intimate experience. Shockingly, I was not that conservative, fearful person any longer, that individual who was brought up to believe that respect and being respected regarding matters of sex and intimacy meant deferring sex until marriage. I was now free to act on my immediate selfish desires without repercussions from anyone. I had reached a point that I was able to express my own sexuality and put aside the guilty feelings I used to have.

The fluidity of expression during our short drive to this glorious and sensuous man's house continued on a physical level the moment we entered his home, which was lovely, well-kept, and showed the evidence of his musicality. I admired this classically trained musician; I might even have been in awe of him. A variety of stringed instruments were strategically placed in corners of his sunlit front living room. Books by varied artists filled the freshly painted shelves. A master of his craft, he was not only an accomplished musician, but also a talented and creative craftsman, I found out later. He made all of those beautifully constructed cellos, banjos, violins, and mandolins.

This was enough to twirl my head into a whirlwind of wonder. What if we joined forces in our artistic endeavors? I loved to create. I was an illustrator who loved drawing and painting. To work alongside someone with a similar passion … wouldn't that be a wonderfully satisfying relationship?

We abandoned polite introductory pleasantries, and the dance of sensual erotic wonder began. Mr. Salsa placed his arm behind my back as if to guide me, and I immediately placed my hand on his leader's shoulder. The characteristics of this salsa dancer influenced me, his partner, when it came to the next moves on this dance floor. The timing and movements were precise, so I knew what the next move would be. He lifted me up onto his freshly made bed, and the feel of the crisp white sheets made me feel as if all this, and what was to come, was a clean and proper act. Was it? I had just met this dancer, but I felt I knew him. It all seemed so familiar and right. The dance was filled with romantic gestures, with caring and sweet over-tones, and the suggestion of possibly long-lasting love. But these are logical and reasonable statements and feelings; at the time the chemicals of love flooded my brain. I really didn't care. This was a lovely and sexual afternoon, and maybe that was all it ever would be with this dancer.

With his extremely large hands softly caressing me, I felt a rush of excitement. He carefully strummed my breast as if I were one of his delicate stringed instruments, one that he had played so often before me. The gentleness from such a large man was so contradictory to what I would have imagined. He was an artist and a good one. Strategically placing each finger around my small and erect nipples, he gently and without hes-itation mounted the very instrument he was performing with. He practiced precision and perfection in every seductive move, gliding those massive fingers toward the lower quadrant of this instrument, all the while holding me with great control. He slipped his middle finger ever so slowly into me, ready to create the melodic sound of lovemaking. My immediate response was of pleasure. This dancer had practiced many times before and was skillful at his craft, anticipating the calculated moves. I felt revealed and ready for the overture. With appropriate finger placement and movement, the orchestra of love began. With great satisfaction and mutual response, the dance and show went on until exhaustion set in and the final reprise happened. As we laid our heads back onto the pillows, a glance and a smile signaled the end of the final movement. The curtains closed. Bravo and encore.

Lovely as the experience was, this would be the one and only time I performed with this dancer. As I discovered with many others, if both partners are not available to practice, either out of a lack of desire or mere impracticality due to distance, it is impossible to begin a dance and think that it will culminate in perfection or, in this case, a long-term relationship. Over the next few years, the moments that were so exciting would be replaced by a few sensual phone messages in the hopes of practicing our instruments again. It was never to happen.

Chapter 9

"You are spam and a liar. Go away."

Those were the words that popped up at me as I returned to my laptop of love. The cold and shocking statement from someone I did not know appeared smack in front of my face. Trying to put that jarring experience aside, I continued assessing the next new page full of viewers for my perusal. I was interrupted by a message:

> "All Caps Annie, where have you been?"

There he was again, my literary critic, the one who slammed me with his disapproval of my use of all capital letters. He probably hadn't found anyone else who would respond to his quirky but clever approach to getting a woman's attention. His message continued:

> Every time I am down I go to my computer and there to greet me is a list of my favorites and best matches and there you are. Must be something that pulls us together. Make your choice. Beer, back rub or diet coke. I

> know it is a hard call, my back is more like
> 4 feet wide and covered with rippling mus-
> cles, well more like lean welts.

How very sad, I thought. He thinks that is cute? Not too cute in my mind. Perhaps he could use a lesson in approaching women successfully when looking for dates online. I decided that I wouldn't be his teacher. After all, I too was a beginning learner in this new game of dancing.

"I just wanna have fun," the tagline read.

Yeah, don't we all. But what does that suggest about this man? Would he make a good companion, a lover, or was he an irresponsible boy who never grew up? I decided to keep reading.

> I live alone, slowly losing my mind. I have a
> beautiful home on the water and every toy
> a guy could want. I want to share my life
> with someone I love. I love to restore clas-
> sic boats and play classic music. Six-one,
> blond hair, hazel eyes, athletic, and toned.
> Divorced, two kids. White, Caucasian. I
> am Dutch. I love chocolate! Last book I
> read: *How to Talk to a Liberal.*

This was one interesting person. I loved him already, especially the fact that he loved chocolate. What could be more perfect? As I looked at his pictures, I was pleasantly surprised to see a gentle looking man with two beautiful daughters and two lovely dogs. Several shots showed a man with many interests: boating, fly fishing in the mountains of Colorado, sailboats, motorcars, and airplanes. I knew that this partner would be fun and brotherly, quick-witted, and a little bit sarcastic. Just up my alley. Having four brothers, I was used to the teasing and banter that accompanies the back and forth rhetoric of infantile male behavior. I lived with it. I was used to being teased and teased back. I decided to begin the dance withMr. Cha-cha.

The cha-cha's name is onomatopoeic, derived from the scrape and the shuffling of the dancers' feet, the rhythmic push from one partner as the other pulls. The dance can be energetic with a steady beat or more sensual with a complex polyrhythm. The modern ballroom version of the cha-cha-cha is a gradual evolution of moves. Such was the evolution of my new partner. As usual, I sent a quick wink and a short note: "LIKED YOUR CUTE AND WITTY PROFILE. TELL ME MORE ABOUT YOURSELF."

The waiting game began. After several days with no answer, I thought, okay, he's not interested. I knew not to get too disappointed when hoping for responses. There may be many reasons for delays: not at the computer, busy at work, out of town? Or possibly he just wanted to play a little game by refusing to show any eagerness in responding. Still, the fear of rejection is always an unpleasant feeling.

With a late night announcement, the computer notified me of a reply. It was Mr. Cha-cha:

> "I build boats. I need your number! I have toys and fly planes." The message included a photo of this man and his toys: a beautifully crafted wooden Chris-Craft boat from the 1950s refurbished to perfection, sailboats, a small ultralight plane, and a Cessna jet.

> "That is the biggest toy plane I have ever seen," I responded with enthusiasm.

> "Hold on, I'll be there before you know it," he replied.

How fun this dialogue was! Here was a gentleman with spirit and a sense of humor that I appreciated. The conversation continued; he came up with a plan.

"Listen to this scheme. You take the ferry across the lake, I will pick you up and we play in my territory for a few days and then I will fly you back." As I pondered this offer, my thoughts were, Oh, he's kidding now. Just a jokester.

"Scheming Mr. Cha-cha, sounds like a plan. But what if we don't like each other? That's a lot of time to be with someone you may not want to around for more than a few hours!"

Not being too keen on spending a first meeting with a stranger on his turf, I suggested he fly to meet me in a neutral territory. I suggest that we could have dinner out.

"Well sometimes you just have to go for it. Besides I already like you. Believe me, if I find I do not like you I will have you home in no time flat. Just three clicks of those ruby slippers. One way or the other we are going to be friends," he wrote back.

"Now that's what I like about you: you're very decisive. And the reference to *The Wizard of Oz* couldn't be more perfect. It is one of my favorites; I love it! I played Auntie Em in the show. Okay, Mr. Planner. Tell me where to go and what to bring. I love an adventure," I said.

"Damn you really are impulsive. Let me sleep on it. Your job is to check the ferry schedule and rates, okay? Don't disappoint me, Auntie Em. I have flying monkeys and I am not afraid to use them. Good night, beautiful," came the response.

"No, *you* are the one that should be responsible for this impulsivity. You better think on it because I am not prepared for any monkeys on my back."

"I will check the ferries. Let's talk on the phone after my homework is complete. I am having fun just thinking about it. Goodnight, my little Dorothy. Ready for the yellow brick road?"

"Yes, this is fun. Maybe flying would be faster—I could hop in my bed and wait for that tornado to whirl me across the waters onto your wonderland. Have a poppy-filled field of dreams . . . Night."

"Google this area. It is a charming artists' community in the heart of cherry and wine growing vineyards."

"Do your homework now."

"Nighty night."

As the week passed, there was little word from the wizard, so I chalked our conversation up to an amusing night of fun-filled, noncommittal banter. I was wrong. The very next day, I received a stern and terse e-mail from Mr. Cha-cha.

"Hold on there, Auntie Em. You are a Democrat? I thought you were an intel-

ligent lady and then I read in your profile
that you are liberal. I am not sure that we are
going to get along. Our ideas may not be in
line with one another. I am disappointed."

After all the back and forth, pushing and pulling of each
other's strings, I was the disappointed one. Thinking that Mr.
Cha-cha was an intelligent, clever, fun-filled individual, I was
taken by surprise to read this terse and heartless message. My
response was a retaliation, but I tried to maintain the tone of
the clever dialogue from the previous evening:

> Good morning, I just read your message
> and my image of you as a rigid galvanized
> Tin Man looking for that heart that is miss-
> ing has replaced the once kind and gentle
> Mr. Wizard. I would like you to prove to
> me that you are wrong. You may be think-
> ing I am the liberal, mindless Scarecrow
> who has little knowledge. I assure you that
> your assumptions couldn't be farther from
> who I am. I would prefer to be the loving
> and kind-hearted Auntie Em. No, I am not
> a staunch Democrat. I prefer to think of
> the word liberal as meaning someone who
> is capable of looking at all sides of the equa-
> tion with an open mind, evaluating what
> is the best scenario in all aspects of life,
> whether political, social, religious and the
> like. An independent thinker, you might
> say. My liberal thoughts revolve around
> that ability to listen, process, assess, and
> make a rational and intelligent decision
> about the issue at hand. That includes not
> making rash, uneducated decisions about
> meeting someone I only know from the
> clicks on our keyboards and a voice, who
> offers assurance that I will be safe and

happy with that decision. I do think that we need to continue our dialogue to get to know each other before researching itineraries for travel. Enough said. Now go back to your rigid shell of metal and ponder.

He wrote back:

Now, now. It seems I hit a soft spot and you are being a bit presumptuous about what I think you think. The truth is you're close but gee whiz, let a guy defend himself, would ya? By the way, did you research any ferry information yet?

After a week of calming down without communication, I felt Mr. Cha-cha was probably not the best individual to continue a cyber relationship with. The dance never really got off the airwaves, so practicing in person would probably never occur.

As I was about to say, "It was fun to imagine the possibilities with you, Mr. Cha-cha, but I wish you the best," another message flew across my page. I never had the chance to write those words as here he was again, pushing forward with clever dialogue to keep me interested.

"Auntie Em, did you finish your homework assignment? Next week would be a great time to visit. The colors are starting to pop already. Good night, my liberal Auntie."

How could I end this comical banter between two people who clearly enjoyed the fun and silliness of it all? The next message read, "Did you forget me already?" Oh my, a sense of guilt filled me. I worried that I would hurt another man's ego, and leave him to pursue another unsuspecting naïve Dorothy. This wizard was good. I did not respond. I needed time to consider the best way to deal with Mr. Cha-cha.

A week passed, and I felt the need to at least respond. After all, Auntie Em was not cold and calculating, nor did I look at things in black and white. The middle grey shades would allow for a new look at this dancer. I certainly didn't want to be that heartless woman of tin. I sent an e-mail.

> No, I have not forgotten my quick-witted Internet friend. How are you on this beautiful, colorful fall day? This good witch Glinda is thinking about hopping into her bubble to float over that vast mass of water that separates us. Are your monkeys in the cage?

This was the last communication for quite some time until he sent me a Facebook friend request. His comment on my beautiful family photo set the tone for a continuation of our dance, which maybe now would continue in person.

In his first message after a month or more, Mr. Cha-cha came up with several new plans. I thought, oh, he hasn't forgotten me. He must have been thinking of new ways to approach me without offending me.

> "New Plan. Three options. (1) I come visit you, and stay until you get sick of me. (2) You drive to Chicago and meet me for a weekend. (3) You take the ferry over, and I pick you up and send you back if we don't like each other."

After a few moments of deliberation, I replied, "I choose number 2."

I was not opposed to Mr. Cha-cha visiting me, but being somewhat conservative regarding dating and being a bit old school, I felt the man should initiate the first meeting. He should go out of his way to meet my needs first. Compromising was a good idea. I did feel that both of us taking a little initiative and meeting halfway would be best. The weekend was decided on. I would have to work this trip around a trip south and also accommodate his schedule so that we could actually finalize our plans. Bad idea! Returning home early, expecting a call or any form of communication to reaffirm our plans to meet, I was left with *no response*. No return phone messages, no Internet banter. Boy, did I feel like a fool. Maybe I was the simple-minded Scarecrow who allowed someone to take advantage of my ignorance? I chose to think of it more as naiveté and vulnerability. I guess I shouldn't have been too surprised. This seemed to be a pattern. This dance was complex, with its many confusing steps, the antagonistic push and pull of our personalities. Why the continual intrigue? He was a curiosity, and he kept me on that virtual dance floor. Was it the anticipation of the next step, or was it the excitement of not knowing where it was going? This partner kept me at arm's length, and never allowed that close bodily connection needed for a successful dance. After several attempts, I did not expect to finish this dance.

Once again, Mr. Cha-cha's pull brought me back onto the floor. He messaged me.

> "It's time to stop admiring each other from
> a distance, my pretty."

"I concur, Mr. Cha-cha. Your move." My reply was quick and to the point.

"Thanksgiving with me and then you take me home for Christmas. Deal?" He pulled in closer.

> "Tempting, but family here for both.
> Do we have to wait for New Years? We
> really don't know that much about each
> other, do we? I think we need to fill in the
> minor details."

Again, closer and closer, he replied, "I know you're special because of my male intuition. You wouldn't understand."

"Anything you want to know about this girl from cyber space?"

"A lot." Love male intuition.

"I have female intuition. I guess that is why we continue to communicate."

"Let's send our intuitions ahead for a TST meeting. What do you think they would say?"

"I am confident that we are both well educated, come from good families, are talented, and are independent people who have a lot to share."

A large and stunning black-and-white photograph from 20 years earlier appeared before my eyes, a portrait of a family of ten. It featured a handsome mother and father with their equally handsome four boys and four girls posed in a relaxed and loving moment in their lives as a family. Wow! This was a physical, virtual confirmation of the many impressions I had of this dancer.

I exclaimed, "See, my intuitive side was so right. Lovely family, and large too."

At this point, I knew we had a common bond. I too was raised in a large family of four brothers and four sisters. How coincidental was that? Odd, to say the least, but so refreshing at that moment. His ability to share his family showed a sensitive side to this jokester. I loved it. I quickly perused my family photos and sent an attachment right back to Mr. Chacha, a family photo of my siblings taken some 20 years past. As I waited for a response, I thought to myself how different communication is when we are relying on instant gratification, just like we did with telephone conversations back in my day.

"A picture of wholesomeness. Is that a word?"

"Sounds correct to me. I will take wholesomeness any day. Thank you," I replied.

"It is getting late, Dorothy. Off to those poppy filled fields for a night of slumber. We shall discuss your trip to visit me later. And yes, you have a hint of maintenance issues. I know I am an expert in detection. But we will work on it together when you come see me."

"You are so wrong about me, very wrong. Now what issues do we need to work on with you? I think you are afraid we are going to like each other. My ruby slippers are ready just in case."

"I already know I like you. Question is, how spontaneous can you be? What are you thinking right now?"

"I can be spontaneous, but can you?"

"With the right motivation, yes."

"You are now my Cowardly Lion and I am that girl with the ruby slippers ready for adventure. You are invited to visit me anytime. As I indicated before, I am an old fashioned girl from that era when the man initiates the first response."

"Okay, I will send my flying monkeys to get you."

"What kind of motivation do you need?"

"A cute blonde."

"Then hop on the wizard's balloon and fly over that lake that separates us. I am going brunette."

"Bullshit … It doesn't really matter."

"Do I have to wait for winter when those poppies are dormant and not quite so hallucinatory?"

"I'm thinking. I'm scared."

"Ha ha I knew it. What are you afraid of?"

"What if we actually fell in love? Not sure I can handle it."

"Awesome!!!"

"Seriously?"

"Just enjoy life, Mr. Cha-cha. Don't let little things like that stop you from meeting someone. I am as homespun as that little farm girl from Kansas. I find you most interesting, and I think you need someone to shake you up."

"Okay, I am sure that it is just a matter of time."

"Get out of that poppy field."

"But I am so sleepy."

"Me as well, funny guy. Go to bed."

"Okay. Good night for now and thank you for that chat. I needed it. And I do like your assertive side."

"See I entered back into your world when you needed me the most. Must be clairvoyant ... thinking about you."

"Serendipity."

"When you get your courage, make a plan—a girl can't wait forever. Snap out of it, as Cher would say. Oh, I love serendipity!"

"Understood."

"Sleep well. I shall be waiting."

"Goodnight sugar plum."

"Sugar plum, that's a new one just in time for Christmas. You know I might be just what the doctor ordered."

One thing I have learned is that we are similar, and those similarities are evident in small personality traits that come out through the back and forth of communication. I usually realized quickly those who I felt at ease with and others who I felt less comfortable with, just by focusing on how we communicated. The conversation could flow with genuine interest, eagerness, joviality, and feeling or it could become awkward and cumbersome, leading to feelings of tension, fear, and apprehension. With some people, I didn't know or care where the conversation was going. I just wanted it to end. There is always a dominant leader in conversation, just as there is a leader in dance. It is always more difficult to take that lead.

Mr. Cha-cha was an antagonist, a negative nelly of sorts, dominant in that he always wanted to have the last word in a conversation, or take that last dance step on the floor. His expectations and his need to create disharmony from the start irritated me, so I was careful not to make the wrong step, always concerned about the leader's approval in hopes that there would be little disciplinary action on his part. Conversations were more fun when he felt in control. He was a taskmaster and relished having the upper hand. He looked for imperfection in order to keep his partner at arm's length, so as not to get too close. Why? I guessed that this dancer was painfully damaged after a divorce, which led to low self-esteem and a lack of confidence. He was defending his weaknesses for fear of another rejection. Bingo.

As our phone calls became more frequent, personal information began to be revealed. After all the pushing and pulling of each other's emotional chains, Mr. Cha-cha opened up about his personal plight. The conversation was disquieting and set a tone for a more intimate partnership. No longer interested in the childlike brother-sister squabbling, he was now allowing me in to his space, albeit for a short time.

"Yeah, I was married for 30 years to the love of my life, and she left me."

Wow, what a confirmation of all that I had suspected. But there was more.

"I had a small stroke, and my rehabilitation was long, leaving me with recurring bouts of depression. I am managing it now with medication, but she couldn't deal with me and all the ramifications of caring for a person with a disability. I am afraid no one would want this burden. I have had to reinvent myself. After a lot of work and soul searching, I left my job and started building things, particularly boats. It has been my sanctuary.

"When I first began this quest of looking for another person to let onto my dance floor, I only searched for those who would provide me with sex. It was unfulfilling. I suppose it may have been due to my insecurity in letting anyone get close. The shell is hardened and the armor is up. Closeness becomes a threat, and I am not able to defend myself."

His honesty was refreshing, but it was sad to know the truth, the real truth about someone. He was hurting and most likely would be spending many years alone. This dance would continue only on the level of a friendship, instead of partnership. As a nurturer, I was a safety net, a sounding board for this once-vital man who has lost the vigor and stamina to carry out any dance. I would have to be content with this friendship, since I had the impression this dancer never wanted to meet to learn the dance of the cha-cha.

Chapter 10

The jive, or the jitterbug, is a high-energy, lively, uninhibited form of swing dance. It's a dance without control, full of improvising and cutting loose and going crazy. This dance may be uncomfortable to perform with a partner at first due to the frenetic, chaotic, unpredictable moves. The technical difficulties need to be mastered. To improve, regular practice is a must so that partners can understand the timing of each other's moves to create a balance.

Life is all about attitude. Attitude sets you apart from the crowd, and for me, keeping a youthful attitude is all about having a little kid inside. People would describe me as funny, passionate, and *energetic*! I strongly feel that if there are the four Cs in a relationship, so it can stand the test of time, those Cs are communication, commitment, chemistry, and compromise.

On my screen was a profile of a very handsome man with a smile that could melt hearts. He was 50 years of age and divorced with two children.

I sent a wink and received a comment from this high energy, happy, extroverted man. We started e-mailing.

> Good morning, good morning, good morning beautiful. You are adorable, and I loved

reading your profile. So you are a tennis player? Let's hit some balls and get to know each other.

Hi Mr. Jitterbug. It's a pleasure to meet you. You have a lovely smile. You look so much like my brother. We could be related. Thank you for your notice and for reading my profile. I realize the age difference may be a deterrent but I assure you I feel 35. Tell me about yourself.

Newly separated, after being married for 15 years. Thought I was married for life but when commitment and trust are lost it hurts a relationship. As you read in my profile I emphasize the 4 Cs. My friends think I am fun, funny, energetic, and trustworthy. I worked in the family wealth management business until I decided to go it alone. I now enjoy the freedom of real estate brokerage, selling high-end homes. I enjoy and have played and taught golf and won many club championships. I was an avid tennis player through high school and college. My favorite memories I cherish were when my children were born ... awesome.

You look perfect. Can we talk? Can we exchange phone numbers?

Our first phone conversation did not start well. A missed call and a voice mail came. In a contemplative, almost angry tone he said. "Annie, just giving you a jingle. You know this would never work. You live three hours away. Even if we were perfect for each other, fell in love, wanted to get married, we are just setting ourselves up for disappointment."

Yikes, what an introduction! I called back, not sure what to think.

"You do realize I am a bit older than you are? Is that a problem? Men of your age seem to be searching for a perfect thirty-something with a killer body."

"No, no, no. My grandmother always said that age does not matter. Always have the kid inside you. Never let that die because then you become old. Think of it this way: when you are a hundred I will be ninety-three. Big deal, huh?"

Yowza, what a great answer. I thought, I have got to meet this guy.

"So if you have already negated the potential for any kind of relationship, why begin the process of communication? I personally don't feel that the three-hour distance is a problem, if there is a desire and determination behind wanting to see someone." My feeling was, at this stage of our lives, why not be adventuresome, experience the moment, and see what happens? We might even like each other. We didn't have to be stuck thinking *long-term*. I wanted to enjoy making a new friend and see where it went. He agreed, so we decided to continue our dance. Going off the site to communicate made it easier to connect more frequently.

Our conversations continued for several weeks, all generalized in nature, usually centered on a golf tournament or tennis match. At the, time the French Open was going on. Mr. Jitterbug messaged me about what he was watching, giving me the play-by-play.

"Federer up 2 sets."
"Djokovic playing out of his mind."
"Serena is so strong."
"Love love love Ana Ivanovic."
"Chris   Evert   makes   ridiculous   comments."

"Rafa is my man. Such an all around player."

That was the content that filled our daily conversations, nothing other than simple, safe topics. He clearly didn't want to be carried away into more in-depth dancing. His messages were quick, unemotional, and uninformative about him personally. I wanted more. More of an in-depth insight into what this person was really thinking. I sensed that this might never happen.

Another call. No hellos, just a comment.

"Your Wisconsin boy in the golf tour is up three shots on the leader board. Happy for him."

Aha, an opening.

"Yes, I am very happy for him. He is a lovely person."

"Fantastic! I was best friends with Payne Stewart. We were roommates at Texas. Great guy and golfer. Went to many tournaments with him. Since you are a tennis player, I don't suppose golf is in your repertoire?"

"I play golf, but it's not a passion for me. My drives are good, my second shots okay, but my chipping and short game needs work. Love to putt. Can I enlist you for a lesson or two?'"

"I'll show you some moves. Of course, of course!"

"I can show you some moves. I can still do the splits." Where on earth did that come from? Back to golf, I thought.

"My former life was consumed with golf. There were many professionals in this golf family, so I lived the game of golf for many years. Several family members toured with the pros, playing in major tournaments including the US Open. I was immersed in this sport. Hey, want to go to the US Open tennis tournament this year?"

"One of my favorite memories was when I was invited to the Open in the box. Maybe? You know we have to go on five dates before we can really get to know one another?"

What exactly did he mean by that?

"Elaborate on that statement, please. Are you a respectable man who respects woman?"

"Of course. It is important to get to know someone and see if there is chemistry. One of my four Cs, remember?"

That was the last I heard from Mr. Jitterbug for some time—a month, to be exact. Maybe he thought our conversations were especially energetic, and needed the time to calm down, reflect, or possibly remove himself totally from his dance partner? Maybe he wasn't ready for any relationship since he was just recently separated and had not fully experienced the grieving process. Maybe he wasn't quite through with the idealized thought of his once-blissful marriage. I did not know, but I was disappointed for sure. As time passed without communication, my desire to keep in touch with the dancer diminished. It seemed like a game, an immature waiting game. Looking too interested could prove to be a deal breaker, especially if one dancer was no longer interested. And yet those very fears could prevent a possible reconnection, and thus, more time would elapse, leaving the potential dancers disenchanted. And the dance would end.

I didn't want that to happen, at least not before I got to know this new dancer. Perhaps we were both contemplating another move, but who would be the first to connect? Mr. Jitterbug once again set the moves in motion. Again it centered on a professional tennis tournament. The phone call came late into the night.

"Hi, Annie. How's my split girl? Federer and Nadal—great match. Are you watching with your new boyfriend from cyberspace?"

Ah, this dancer wanted to continue. The interest was still hot, or maybe lukewarm. New boyfriend? This jitterbugger was unclear on how to proceed with the relationship dance. He was spinning a little out of control, but at least he opened the door enough for me to catch him. Now I was the pursued, but in the lead position. I would have to calmly coax him back in to begin again at step one.

"Well, hello again, sweet Mr. Jitterbug. How have you been and how is your family?" Clever, I thought, to pursue a subject near and dear to his heart. It was not a forceful move, just enough guidance to make him feel safe enough to want to continue.

"Good, good. I've missed you, split girl. Federer is smoking Nadal. Why not come and visit this weekend? I will be the planner."

Hm, now what? Should I eagerly make myself available? Would a yes indicate to him that I had been waiting for him and put all other dances on hold? Probably.

"Really, you want me to come visit for the weekend?'"

"Yes. Bring a bag. You are not driving home."

As much as I wanted to feign indifference, I also didn't want to have a repeat waiting game as before.

"Yes, I would like that. I love a planner and welcome your ideas fully. What's first on the agenda, Mr. Jitterbug?"

"I would like to take you to the art museum in Milwaukee. They have a new exhibit of Impressionist painters. I thought you might like that. We could meet for a quick bite to eat downtown. First, I will investigate the area and fill you in on all of the details soon. Sound good, Annie?"

"Sounds awesome. I can't wait. It will be wonderful to finally meet. What should the dress code be? Casual, formal? I am game for anything. You decide, and I will accommodate."

"Absolutely casual, babycakes. Oh, and bring your tennis racquet. We could hit a few balls at the club. I want to check your form on the court."

"Babycakes, that's real cute. Never been called that before. Casual attire is perfect for me. I have always been a jeans and tee shirt kind of girl. I will bring my tennis bag. Watch out, I can place my shots and running is my specialty. I'll chase all your balls down or at least try, even at my age."

"I am sure you can, babycakes."

With GPS in hand and my overnight bag packed with my silky nightie and change of clothes, I couldn't help but wonder, what am I thinking? This is all too much too soon. Would this constitute a fifth date—after a luncheon, then the art museum, tennis match, and another night of dining? Will that evening be the date when we could experience intimacy and romance?

We had not practiced our dance. How would this highly energetic, fascinatingly interesting, smart, handsome man respond on an intimate level? The crazy attraction for me was just that. The laughter and fun exchanges on the phone were so addicting. I was hooked on him like any psychedelic drug. He had a clever, optimistic outlook on life, and this was a hallucinogenic draw for me. Here was a kid in a grown man's body, one who didn't behave according to the social norms of modern day life. He was that wild, uncontrolled dancer with energy never to be harnessed. Anticipation and excitement were the dominant emotions in my mind for the days before our scheduled first meeting. Fantasizing about what might happen became thrilling enough.

The day arrived and, prepping and primping, I made sure that I lived up to all the high expectations of someone I had never met. Sure, he reassured me that the age difference did not matter as long as I had a youthful spirit. Wearing my tight-fitting faded jeans with low-slung boots complemented by my standard casual buttoned-down white blouse, I thought I looked casual but elegant. I was ready to take that dip with a dancer who would surely spin me around the first time on the floor of love. I better hold on tight; this was going to be one wild ride. I knew it. I could feel it. I made the two-hour drive with a mix of apprehension and enthusiastic anticipation, rationalizing that I was a woman of age and finally free to create a little adventure in my once-mundane, conservative, and frankly quite boring life. "Just go for it!" Everyone needs to learn a new dance.

My Bluetooth rang, and there was that exclamatory voice saying, "Where are you? What kind of wine do you like? I am going to the market. Do you like cheese, my Wisconsin girl?" A somewhat condescending, yet cute little dig at my Midwest accent.

"Anything you so desire. You decide. Ten minutes to arrival time."

"Cannot wait, babycakes!"

As we approached our destination, parking was an issue, and the gentleman guided me to an open spot, and then stepped out of his car and directed traffic so that I could parallel park. What a kick. Who does that? Very sweet, I thought to myself, but once again, he's an individual who does not follow the norm. I took the spot. Waiting in my car in front of the little bistro that he chose for our first meeting, I glanced in my side view mirror, and there he was, sprinting down the road to greet me at the door. With his broad smile and beautiful white teeth, I saw him as a youthful, spirited kid, wearing a grey-green tee shirt with a logo of the Salty Dog Cafe, baggy jeans, and flip flops. His disheveled, slightly graying hair was full, thick, and long. He had deep-set brown eyes that twinkled with every smirk he made. With a grand bowing gesture, he opened the door as if I were the queen entering a ballroom for a night of grandeur.

"Annie, you're gonna love this place. They have the best sandwiches. Order here, and I'll get a booth upstairs."

As he once again sprinted up the stairs, I was second-guessing my decision to come. He was not as I expected. Cute for sure, but oh such a mess. A hot mess. He didn't do much to impress me with his appearance or clothes, considering it was a first date. He was more suited to sit on a beach somewhere, eating hotdogs from a vendor. The pictures that were posted on his profile conflicted with how he presented himself now. Having had so many conversations, I did feel I knew him better than as if it were a first date, so I figured it would be interesting, if nothing else. I would be happy to sit back and observe this spirited dancer, as he showed me those moves that would be sure to delight and entertain me.

With sandwiches delivered via a conveyor system to the second floor, we gathered our drinks, mine a lemonade, and his a draft beer. We looked at each other and began to laugh.

"So you are my split girl? Whatcha think?" He slowly opened his arms, bowing to reveal a young silly boy of a man.

"Give me some time, will ya? I need to check on your table manners first."

Here we go again, I thought: quick and quirky, unemotional dialogue. Not wanting to be the first to fall or make that wrong step. The cute remarks continued throughout the lunch. It was fun and lighthearted. The first date and dance was complete, and we were on to the second date and dance for further review to decide if we wanted of a third or fourth.

On to the art museum. Now this was a familiar place for me to shine. I loved art and took a number of art history courses in my day. As we walked through the bright sunlit halls of this most modern gallery, Mr. Jitterbug once again was quick to move. He jumped from one art exhibit to the next, commenting all the while on various master oils from the 18th century. Comical for sure. With great imagination, he made funny references to the painters and what they were thinking in their studies of the nude model. The figures and the colors were muted and unspecific, but Realism was not his preference anyway. The distortion of landscapes and figures was more his style; he understood the visually disproportionate images. As we walked and talked, he was the catalyst, I was the respondent. Much of my reaction was in laughter. He was an out-of-control, untamable stud skirting around his filly in hopes of corralling her into the third round of dancing.

After several hours of side-splitting moments at the museum, we were both ready to find a quiet little pub for a beverage or two. We decided on a local tavern that offered a variety of beers. Not being much of a beer drinker, I opted for a glass of pinot grigio. Sitting across from each other on tall wooden bar stools did not seem very romantic. It was much like being with the buddies at a post-athletic event. Shoot the shit, have too much to drink, make a fool of one's self. Yes, this was the third date, and as much fun as the first two were, this one seemed less exciting. Watching Mr. Jitterbug down three beers in succession, I began to wonder if he had a drinking problem. His demeanor changed a bit, from highly energetic to more subdued, and less interested. I was his drinking buddy for the night, and his idea of a fourth and fifth date diminished.

On my second glass of pinot grigio and his fourth beer, I thought this might be an opportune time to ask how he felt about our date. ,

"How are you feeling about our day together?" We were both, needless to say, feeling few inhibitions at this point, so an honest answer would be much easier to handle.

"Awesome, Annie, I think you're great. I had a ball today. I want to see you again. Aren't you coming over tonight? It's getting late and you really shouldn't be driving in the condition you're in. I insist, babycakes. You can have my son's room. The sheets are clean. We could get up in the morning. I will make you some coffee with my special bacon and eggs and then we could play a little tennis at my club, have a lovely dinner downtown, and then you decide if you want to be on your way."

The mania began again. He didn't come up for air. I thought to myself, Slow *down*, take a breath, relax. But the energy increased until I finally interrupted to say, "I really had a wonderful time with you, Mr. Jitterbug, and thank you for all those plans you arranged. But I really must get home, and you should go home as well. Get some sleep. It has all been very eventful."

"Okay, split girl … but I worry about you driving."

"I am just fine. I will worry about you driving home. Are you going to be all right?"

"Me? Are you kidding? I am sober. It takes more than four of these. Thanks, Annie. I really enjoyed your company. But damn, you live so far away. I know we are going to be disappointed."

"I am not disappointed. I am so happy that we could meet and discover a little more about each other. If you are interested and you don't feel it's too far, I would love to have you come visit me. My turn to show you around. I will be the planner. Our fourth date?"

"Wisconsin girl … better get the brats and cheese ready cuz I am coming to town." At that moment, the bartender asked if he could take our picture. I said yes, of course. Handing him our phones, he shot a few frames. We embraced and had a moment of closure. The picture would be our connection for months to come, the only piece of evidence that we each existed and a way to remember the moments we experienced together. "Drive carefully. Bye for now, babycakes," he said.

Oh what a relief! A relief that this whirlwind of a day was over. A relief that I was returning to my safe and calm environment without all the stimuli. I needed to rest. Amazing the amount of energy one exerts when with a partner who emits chaos. I was tanked—ready for bed and alone, thankfully.

I was not surprised that days and weeks passed with no word from my Mr. Jitterbug. I was okay with that, but still wondered why. Did he not find me attractive? Was I not his type? Was I too old and easygoing? Perhaps he was looking for someone who could equal him in nervous energy. I was not that partner, and never would be. Even knowing this, I felt a connection to Mr. Jitterbug, and the drug of excitement had not worn off yet. I did want more. He was so darned adorable. Nothing boring about this dancer. He certainly would provide a lifetime of entertainment, even though it might be all too exhausting for any partner. I decided I would wait and let the chips fall where they may. The photo was our bond for now. Glancing at the memory of that day and the adorable man behind that devious smile was keeping me in this dance. Maybe a little gambling was in order with this dancer; the addiction may have been just beginning. Playing my cards right was profitable for sure, not in a monetary sense but in the sense of waiting until this partner would make the next move. He always did.

"Annie, I need a date for a pool party. Want to come see me?'"

Geez, poor guy. He really didn't know how to get a woman's emotional attention. I wasn't sure he had a romantic side to him. Should I be his date? No, not this time. It was my turn to make up the itinerary, and so I respectfully declined, making up some excuse that I had a tennis tournament or something, but asked if he would like to come for the day the following week. I would take him out for lunch, show him around my turf, and possibly get in a round of golf. It was my turn to impress. I did so hope he would accept. I really wanted to see him again and practice where we left off. Hopefully the date would on a different note and we would design new steps in our dance of delirium. With a quick click of the keyboard, he said, "Yes yes, I would love to see you. I will bring my clubs. You know you are the only woman I have a photo of in my phone. We look great together."

"Perfect." The dance card was still hot off the press and we had plenty of work to do to get this dance started on the right steps. I wanted to complete this dance. I thought he did too. That photo, an image of a positive first meeting, kept our interest alive. We could now add more to our respective photo galleries, fantasizing about the possibilities.

It was a hot day in late July. I was prepared for a sultry and different beginning to our dancing, hoping that the hyperactive Mr. Jitterbug would be less exhausting on this date, more willing and able to learn the dance of romance. I was willing to let him in on my more normal pace of action. I did not want a reactionary connection, but one that would be complementary and more meaningful in really understanding an individual on a deeper level. I was all too aware of the superficial personality of this dancer, but I needed to peel back that first meaningless layer of his soul. I hoped the man beneath would be different.

I was prepared to look strong, confident, and beautiful. Deciding on a sleeveless black V-neck tee shirt and tight-fitting white shorts and my flip-flops, I knew that this would create a comfortable sense of familiarity for this very casual partner. The day would include a light lunch at a downtown bistro in the heart of this beautiful capital city, with its lush gardens and flowers and two glorious lakes, a backdrop fit for any Hollywood movie. This was sure to impress if he was able to slow down enough to take in any of it. Mr. Jitterbug had the restless energy of a caged animal; I hoped this time to release the caged animal and give him a sense of freedom, which might lead him toward an inner calm. I would be that lion tamer.

The doorbell rang. He showed up in that same Salty Dog green tee shirt and a nice pair of baggy light beige shorts, minus the flip-flops. He looked energized and ready for an adventure. He offered me a jar of honey in his hand, saying, "A little honey for you, babycakes. My brother has a honey harvest every year, and I have a supply to sweeten a continent."

I hated honey, but what a sweet gesture.

"Why, thank you. That was very sweet of you. Come in. Come in. I want you to meet my daughter."

"Hello, hello. Good to meet you. Where are you off to this fine summer day? You are as cute as your mom described. What grade are you in? What are you studying? Do you have a boyfriend? Are you a golfer and tennis player like your mom? Want to come to lunch with us? I would love to have you join us."

Oh no, here we go again. His foot on the accelerator was getting heavier and heavier. Would he let up on that foot to receive a response, or was he going to crash and burn with me alongside him?

With little hesitation, my very personable and delightful daughter sensed his anxiousness and tried to diffuse it and gently ease that foot off the pedal.

"I have heard a lot of lovely things about you, and it is a pleasure to finally meet. What are you two planning for the day? I appreciate your offer, but I do have plans today. You enjoy. It is going to be lovely!"

"You are a doll! Just like your mother. I see that you come from special stock. It is all about the genes, and you have some good ones. Beauty, presence, charm, and clearly intelligence."

My, what a charmer this man was. Clearly he was brought up with the appropriate social graces. I liked that. I liked that a lot. Just another magnetic draw to keep my interest evolving. And he was oh so handsome—a picture of wholesomeness, of familiarity. He reminded me of a brother, part of the family that was so dear to my heart. He could fit in perfectly.

"So show me around, Annie. Time's a-wasting, babycakes."

"Babycakes? All righty! My chariot awaits. Are you driving?'

"Of course. Lead the way, and I will be your chauffeur."

On the short drive to the restaurant, I pointed out various important landmarks in hopes he might be interested. He seemed engaged and not on a whirlwind of escalating manic behaviors.

His impulsiveness was at bay for the time being. The day included a tour of the capitol and the university in all of its intellectual and historical excitement, without the hustle and bustle of the young students as when school was in session. It was a more subdued time. On the visit to the Memorial Union, taking a seat by the serene waters of the adjacent lake, we were able to connect on a visceral level. The lake was a calming factor, which allowed for level-headed, free-flowing conversation without the interruption of the demons that may have inhabited his ever volcanically erupting mind. It was pleasant and meaningful. We were able to get to know each other on a level conducive to healthy attraction. Finally, goal accomplished, it was time for another photo opportunity. With arms around one another, we added two more pictures to our book of memories.

Then I introduced him to my golfing skills and enlisted a few lessons from this competent and confident golfer. After all, that was his passion, so why not focus on what was important to him? He changed into more appropriate golfing attire, donning a white broad-brimmed golf cap and a lovely collared lime-green shirt with crisp, light cream, below-the-knee golf shorts that put him in a league with the professionals in my eyes. He was a darling! Setting our clubs on the cart, we set off for a few hours of athletic investigation. I would be able to assess this partner and see if he fit all my important prerequisites for a partner. Having grown up in a very athletic family in which sports were important, athletic ability was one quality that I looked for in a match. Every swing and choice of clubs for first and second shots and chips and putts showed an intelligent and much calmer individual than I had observed before this. Mr. Jitterbug showed perfect form and precision in every aspect of the game. Certainly, it was a game he knew well. I was mesmerized and charmed by this athlete. He fit the bill. I could stay here all day. But the time wouldn't allow it. After nine holes, the day was getting late and the sun began to slowly move toward the horizon in blazing orange. As we approached the last hole, we both marveled at the beauty of the day as well as how much we had enjoyed each other's company. The day was a winner, to be sure.

As he chauffeured me back to my house, I invited him in for a drink before he left. He declined, as he had a three-hour drive and his dog was probably bursting to go out. I started to say "I understand. Thank you for…" but at that moment, he unexpectedly took me into his arms, and with a quick move, we locked lips for what would be only an instant. With a glance into my eyes, he attempted a second kiss, hoping it might be more affectionate and meaningful. It was again too quick and without the kind of passion I wanted with this new dance partner. He pulled back again, I thought with disappointment. I too was disappointed. Wiping the lipstick that remained on his lips, he remarked, "You don't look anything like your picture." And he said, once again, "You know we are setting ourselves up for complete disappointment. It's hard when we live so far from one another."

I couldn't argue with that. All I could think of was the disappointing kiss and the slam of my photos. I was irritated at his attack, and all I wanted to do was either defend myself or crawl back into the safe haven of my personal space. That is exactly what I did. This fourth date didn't turn out to be what I was hoping for. That fifth date would probably never come to fruition.

I didn't expect to be practicing the jitterbug anymore. It just was not the dance of my dreams, nor was I comfortable with the uncertainty in the moves. They were all without pattern, and I needed regularity, consistency, and desire from my dancer. Who out there would be able to provide me with a partnership of healthy proportions? I resigned myself to crossing this dance off my list. I was okay with that. I wasn't feeling it at this point. I didn't need irritation and inconsistency in my life now. I would never hear from this dancer again, or so I thought.

A few weeks passed, and I must admit with some sadness that I was not able to make that connection with someone who appealed to me on so many different levels. It was grief of small proportions, but a loss nonetheless. Having accepted this loss, I was shocked to receive a bewildering message from my hot mess of a friend.

> Hey Annie. Why don't you come down to see me at my place this time? I will put some steaks on the grill, baked potatoes and cheese for my Wisconsin girl? Bring some tennis clothes, we can play at my club, doubles with my friends. They are going to love you.

Oh no! I thought. The roller coaster is set to begin again. Should I jump on this emotional ride of ups and downs and spins and turns? After a few days of deliberation and with great hesitation, I responded with a quick and calm:

> Sure. When?

> Annie! Next weekend. The kids are with their mother and weather should be fantastic. Can't wait to see you.

What? He can't wait to see me? I kind of doubted those sentiments. If he really was interested, there would have been communication all along the way. I had finished grieving his loss, and now he was putting me through that grinder again. No waiting chariots this time. I decided to meet him again purely out of curiosity. Would there be a different kind of connection? I doubted it, but it was too late to back out now. I would explore the possibility of a friendship more on a brotherly level. After all, kissing someone who resembles a brother was a bit sick.

The fifth date? Possibly? What unexpected moves would I be surprised with this time around the dance floor? Keeping a steady foot and open mind, I would prepare myself for whatever might happen. I would keep both feet on the ground, literally and figuratively.

The drive didn't seem long at all. The positive feeling of anticipation of seeing Mr. Jitterbug again confirmed my continued interest in practicing with this dancer. I wanted to see this through, no matter what the consequences. As I entered a gated community with its lavish gardens engulfing beautiful, stately homes, I couldn't help but think of the contradiction between this tee-shirted, baggy-jeaned, flip-flop-wearing casual guy with few social graces and this very conservative, well-groomed community. How did he fit in? He was an outcast maybe, defiant and rebellious in love and life for sure, which was kind of sexy to me, as a once hippy artist coming out of the free-spirited 1960s era of free love, bra-burning, the women's movement, pot-smoking, and antiwar activism. I got it. I understood it all too well.

As I turned onto the maple tree-lined street of large red-bricked homes, there he was, my hot mess, scruffy-haired, tanned and toned, wearing another casual, logoed tee shirt, the same old light-colored khaki shorts and, of course, those damned flip-flops. I could see a young school-aged boy throwing a football back and forth. This must be his son? He looked to be around 10 or 11, with short blond buzzed hair and the cutest dimpled smile, much like his dad. With grand gestures and direction, Mr. Jitterbug began to guide me into his driveway as if he were on an airline crew motioning with those orange sticks to assist a plane parking at a gate. I emerged from my cockpit and expected a hello or a hug, but instead, all I received was a short introduction to his son and a gesture to go inside, he would follow.

Entering his home opened the door to another chapter of the history of this potential partner. Strategically placed on the freshly painted white walls were a series of black-and-white photographs of his two cherished children. He was a family man who adored his children. It was a warm and safe environment, filled with exquisite pieces of antique furniture interspersed with modern chairs and Persian rugs. Eclectic but lovely. On the other walls, he exhibited expensive works of well-known artists' watercolors, oils, and lithographs. I imagined that these grand pieces once adorned the walls of an even grander home at one point, and now they were left to be showcased in smaller, less exquisite surroundings. The scent of vanilla filled the air, and I found ginger pumpkin bread along with imported cheeses and crackers placed on a tray in the dining room. He did this for me. What a lovely gesture. My thoughts turned to this now broken family, much like mine, an affluent and respected and admired family of four now torn apart by actions he could not control. His life and mine were turned upside down. We were both once committed to creating a family that was to remain together for a lifetime, but we had lost this normalcy. I knew his sense of calm and contentment were gone. Avoiding the pain, he began to spin out of control. I needed to help him stop his dizzying revolutions of despair.

Uncontrollably pacing, Mr. Jitterbug seemed on edge. Here he was, allowing another woman, a possible replacement for his wife, to meet his son, and he was not so sure how to handle the situation. With motherly instincts, I immediately approached his son with compassion and genuine interest, inquiring about his love of sports. He instantly took to the conversation and filled me in on his baseball accolades. Perfect, I thought. This is a subject I knew and lived with for my years growing up with four brothers, one of who played professional baseball. As our conversations about sports, school, and favorite subjects continued, I wondered where in the heck my dance partner had gone. Hearing a stern voice outside, I saw him trying with frustration to corral his little fluffy dog, named Liesl. How funny, a dog named after one of the characters in *The Sound of Music,* my favorite movie of all time. At that moment, I felt like Liesl, 16 going on 17; baby was I naïve. No matter our age, we are all vulnerable to what may be unknown. This would surely be a day of vulnerable moments for both of us.

After driving his son to his mother's home, a grieving father showed through his outward demeanor. As we dropped off one piece of the now scattered family puzzle, Mr. Jitterbug was angry, and his tone was unpleasant when speaking of his ex-wife. She was to be married to another man, and he had not finished his grieving. A man stuck in the angry stage was not who I wanted to see. The possibility of moving forward with a new and different partner would be impossible for him for now. I understood this, but he did not.

After the hurricane of emotions settled down, we decided to return to his home and enjoy a glass of wine, along with those delicious treats that had been left on the table. And with that, a shout exploded from his mouth, "That bitch of a dog. She's probably eating all the things I left on the table. That damn dog."

Immediately I became a bit frightened. This was how he reacted to something so benign? Would his anger be projected onto anyone female? Oh brother, I better not get too analytical, I thought. It would ruin the day. I calmly reassured him that he shouldn't worry about it, and with a flip of a switch, his behavior became less volatile. I was relieved. All that anxiety over nothing, I thought. The plate of cheese and crackers was intact, and so was Liesl, sitting quietly in the cushy armchair, waiting for her master to return. His volatile emotions proved to be exhausting for both dancers. With two glasses of merlot, we hoped to ease the tension and open up those vulnerabilities. We toasted to a day of fun and discovery.

As we felt our inhibitions dissipate, there was a glimmer of romance from my new dance partner. A few under the breath compliments on my beauty came as a shock. He told me, "You look beautiful today."

A return to playfulness ensued. The quiet of that ever-spinning wheel was a welcome surprise. Beneath the frustration of the changes in my partner's new, unexamined life was a desire to connect more deeply; he just didn't know how. Even though the approach is sometimes more important than the outcome, he was always headed for that outcome, forgetting all that is required to get there. His approach was infantile; he needed to be retaught. I needed to be clear that I was not interested in playing games with him. His grandmother's words kept resonating within him: never give up that inner child. The trouble was that instead, he acted like that child, a Peter Pan wannabe—never to grow up. I was Wendy for a night, a night filled with a Neverland of childish play.

"Come on, baby, let's take a bike ride around town. You can use one of the kids' bikes. The tires are pumped. I am going to escort you into a wonderland of the unknown."

Hopping on to the touring bikes, we jetted through the streets of his glorious neighborhood. After what seemed like miles and miles of road, we found ourselves trailing down a dark, overgrown, tree-lined path. The air was damp as we entered this dark and desolate environment, free from homes as well as people. It was beautiful yet eerie. Where were we going? I was feeling the cold set in as the sun began to disappear, taking with it the warmth and light that gave me a sense of comfort and safety. I was venturing into the unknown. Was I with someone who would shift in behavior like the changing of the winds, calm and peaceful one minute and violent and destructive the next? Fear came over me as we hopped off our bikes in this secluded area of large trees and dark paths that lead to who knows where.

Taking my hand, he led me to a cliff overlooking a fast-moving creek set deep into the ravine. In order to reach the water, we had to cleverly, and with skill, navigate the steep and unstable cliff. With sure feet and a bit of reservation, I handled the task without complaint. On the way down, Mr. Jitterbug stumbled a little and stopped to get his bearings. Noticing a fallen tree branch, more like a tree trunk, he quickly began to shear off the smaller branches and stuff them into the little backpack he had slung over his shoulder. Scraping the birch bark from the tree, he piled a stack full into the front pouch of his backpack. What was he doing? All that swept through my imaginative mind was, *Is he a serial murderer?* Is he going to knock me senseless and bury me in this godforsaken place? I could become a Lifetime movie, one of those unsolved murder mysteries. I remembered observing his anger toward his ex-wife and his dog. Did he want revenge on the woman who scorned him? I could possibly be his victim, the recipient of all that pent-up anger.

With all that swirling in the back of my head, I continued to follow. A ray of light appeared ahead, an opening, and finally, there was land. After the journey from the top of the cliff with unsettled footing, we had landed on sure ground. As I took a deep breath, that breath turned to breathlessness. The end of the long and arduous trail of anxiety and fear opened to a sight that could be described as a heaven: a huge body of blue-green sparkling water. Lake Michigan. The waves were glistening in the reflection of the moving light beams, bright and magical. The smell of fresh pure air filled my senses. Once again, the dance took an unexpected turn. The moves went from high anxiety and craziness to balance, smoothness, and synchronization—what a relief. I let the air of calm take over my very tense body. Grabbing my hand, Mr. Jitterbug pulled me to the fire pit that had been frequented by many that came before us. This was not such a secret place after all. Maybe it was his place of solitude, his place of safety. I was welcomed into his sanctuary.

As he prepared the fire with all of those tree branches and pieces of birch bark collected along the way, I felt foolish in thinking that there may have been something more sinister in his thoughts toward me. With the fire ablaze, we sat side by side in the warm sand of the shoreline, and from his little backpack he brought out a corkscrew and a bottle of port wine. We would continue quenching our thirst with sweet nectar from the earth. Watching the sun slowly dip behind the blue-watered horizon, he gently wrapped his arms around me to keep in the warmth for a little while longer. Knowing we had a long journey back to civilization, he actually slowed down enough to feel the chill himself. His body wasn't in full motion anymore. The contradiction between fire and water, calming waves of the endless blue waters fighting the angry flames of the roaring blaze of the energetic, volatile fire reminded me of the juxtaposition within this person's emotional, chaotic psyche.

Recognizing the daylight wouldn't be around much longer, and needing it to guide us through this land of enchantment, we packed up and forged on through partial darkness, slipping along the cliff's edges. We finally reached flatland, and hopped on our bikes for the hard-pedaling trek to his house. It was energizing and fun. I was Wendy, and Peter took me to Neverland.

Warming inside and washing the sand from our respective bodies, Mr. Jitterbug offered me a large, oversized sweatshirt to put over my light tennis jacket. This day was not over. With another glass of hearty cabernet in hand, we exited to his large and private backyard. There were four large Adirondack chairs placed strategically around a self-made fieldstone fire pit. He led me to a chair that would be best for warming by the fire. With a flurry of energy, once again Mr. Jitterbug was in motion. Placing and rearranging the stones around the fire pit, he began to create a wall of stones higher and higher on one side while leaving the front side low and easily visible for fire viewing. Genius, I thought. This would protect the flames from the wind blowing them into the chairs. With amazement, I was watching a worker bee fashion a geometric hive of stone. I felt like the queen. Finished! Now it was time to enjoy the evening with wine, music, and conversation.

Songs played that warmed my heart, music that transported me to a place that brought back pleasant memories of growing up. He chose music from the '60s through the '80s, mostly Kenny Loggins, The Association, Gary Puckett & The Union Gap, Dan Fogelberg, Phil Collins, and his favorite,

Dave Brubeck, with the classic jazz sound of drums and piano. Music was another common bond that brought us together.

This was the interlude to a night of unexpected discoveries. He jumped from his seat and stoked the fire, shooting a quick glance my way. It was dark that night, but the sky was filled with the light of the stars and the vastness of the universe.

"You look beautiful under the stars," he said quietly and quickly.

Warmth and happiness filled my heart.

"Thank you," I said.

I was dancing in the stars at that moment. He opened up.

"Life is filled with those special moments that we take with us to relive and expand on. This is one for me, being here with you; the other is a moment that would equal this one. The Perseids meteor shower comes only once a year, and I was able to witness this great wonder of the world. The spectacle was nothing short of having died and gone to Heaven. We should experience something like that together. If you lived nearer, we could have a great time together. I could see us traveling to Florida for winters, playing tennis, golf, and being just great together! But we can't. Do you have any idea how that frustrates me?"

It was an honest moment of real vulnerability from this dancer; yet maybe it was the calm before the emotional storm? I better respond in kind, I thought.

"Yes, I do enjoy everything about you. We seem to have so much in common."

With that, he pulled me from my oversized chair and swung me close to his taught and tanned body. With my right hand in his left, he reached around my back to draw me so close to his body; I lost my footing. Instantly, I grabbed onto his back with my left hand, and we were ready for the dance to begin. Starting off with surefooted movement back and forth, he drew me in even closer, face to face. The cold air showed the breaths exhaled with each move. Thrusting his body forward and then pulling mine back, we embraced for what seemed like an eternity. It was a lovely, warm, and touching embrace. With a sweet kiss to my shivering lips, he peered into my eyes and looked away almost in frustration, thinking that I could never be in his life. All those preconceived obstacles within his mind were blocking him from seeing our potential. He kissed me again. I could sense a strong desire from this partner, but also a resistance that prevented him from knowing what the next move should be. As quickly as this moment began, it ended; the push away began. With a fling of his left arm, he swung me around in circles, returning back to square one, embracing again. With precision, he opened his stance, casting me off to the corner of darkness like an angler with rod, awaiting that bite from the catch of the day, then slowly reeling me back in to wait for the next casting. The pattern was consistent and rhythmic and fun. The music switched from fast to slow, and so did we. Swaying to the melodies of "How Deep Is Your Love" by the Bee Gees, we were both sent into another solar system, a different dimension. It was all so magical. When he placed his beautifully large hands gently on the back of my neck, all I could do was respond by wrapping my arms round his torso, low enough to feel the top of his lower spine. We were becoming a different pair of dancers now, practicing into the night.

The night of exploration was beginning. Examining one another, hoping for that chemical desire to take hold for that fifth date, we patiently waited. Could it be possible that two individuals with very different personalities and approaches to life were compatible? He had swept me off this dance floor with such accuracy. I felt it was possible he would be just as competent in the bedroom.

The music stopped. I retreated to my oversized Adirondack chair. My new dance partner was not ready for that next step.

With the prowess of a tiger hunting at night for his tigress, he swiftly dashed off into the house. Moments passed, and when he reentered the lair, my tiger presented me with his prey—an unexpected delight—a mind-altering stash of aromatic weed. In front of me were neatly rolled white paper joints filled with grass. I hadn't seen one of those since the 1960s. Inviting. Usually, I was a prude and always conformed to the norm, never breaking any conventional laws, but not tonight. I was ready to relive those fun moments of yesteryear. My new dance partner was corrupting me, and I liked it. With a few tokes underway, memories flooded my now not-so-lucid memory bank of those college days sitting in abhorrent apartments with green shag carpets, beads hanging in doorways, giving the inhabitants some semblance of privacy. The warm sensation filled my vacant brain, dizzying me, altering all rational perception of what was going on around me. And, the *not* caring! The calm resonated from every synapse within my electrical system that was trying to connect, but left without that spark. I sat for what seemed like hours, staring into the vast black universe, imagining myself sitting on one of those brilliant white specks in the deepness of space. I was dancing in the stars, oblivious to my dance partner. The revolutions within my inner solar system left me vulnerable to those outside observers. I was helpless. This dancing tiger left me powerless. I would surrender all will to this king of the universe. The brilliant stars would guide me to something I was not prepared for at all.

Mr. Jitterbug's den of iniquity followed. He led me into his private mating ground. I felt helpless and without recourse. I was still in that land of hallucinogenic mindlessness. Powerless.

As we lay side by side, I felt like a passive, almost comatose tigress lying obediently next to her now-restless mate. He wanted that dance of mating to begin.

The untamed animalistic performance began, void of sensuality warmth and or caring. I became a ritualistic offering to his unleashed madness. Our naked bodies were forcefully slammed together. I couldn't help but notice those dark, blank, emotionless eyes. The fire had burned out. That sparkle was lost, and his eyes were without life now.

Reaching into the bedside table, he pulled out an opaque red bottle filled with a substance that he slathered quickly over his stimulated organ. Without hesitation, the thrusting and emotionless moves of degradation began again. The confusion of my altered state was dissipating. The air was clearing, and once again, that fear set in. This would be the third time today

I felt afraid of this man. How would I get out of this mess? Should I succumb to this dancer, only to have a memory of my role in our fifth date as an unfulfilled participant in what seemed like a demoralizing act?

When he flopped on his back, completely exhausted from meeting those carnal needs, I felt relief for the moment, contemplating the entire day. I wondered how one could feel so much pleasure and at the same time feel anguish and displeasure being with one individual. This certainly was an unstable dance. Could this tiger be tamed? Was I willing to try to brave his roar? I would wait for his next cry for help. I would not enlist my resources to force him onto any dance floor. If and when he was ready to attempt another go around, I would be available. Foolish, maybe, but I was not a quitter. I needed to see this dance until the end.

Two months later, I exhausted all hope that this dancer would want to rehearse once more. I felt that as time moved forward, we would both find others more suited to fill our dance cards of love. I was correct. During a trip to visit family, I was surprised to receive another phone message. With a grand proclamation, he exclaimed, "Annie, I have found the love of my life, but she is married."

Why would he feel the need to call me to tell me this? It wasn't the most pleasant of information for someone who thought at one point we might have a connection. Perhaps he had been looking at our photo gallery. I continued to inhabit a small space within his mind, which made me feel somewhat special. Once again, I felt a sense of being let down, and sorrow for a possibly permanent loss. His call actually allowed me to let go and move toward someone who would provide for me that secure calm and mutually respectful relationship, a new star to explore in this grand universe of love. I wished him well and proclaimed my happiness for him, all the while aching inside.

My dance card had one remaining dance to fill. This time, I would be careful about whom I selected. Maybe.

Chapter 11

The very last dance request on my card was the Viennese waltz. This dance is slow and deliberate, as each step is enunciated with emotion and drama. The extended hand envelops one partner into the leader's form. The warm embrace sets the tone for an exciting moment of wonderment. The slow rhythm of the music catapults the dancers into a time when age was of little consequence, and soft whispers wipe away the emotionless years of relationships. Was it possible that this final dance could heal my soul?

It started with a wink and a comment on one of my profile photos:

"A vision of beauty and grace."

A lovely comment from an unlikely source: this match was not in my age or demographic specifications. Who was this 44-year-old man viewing a profile of a woman many years his senior? The flattery did not go unnoticed, and I decided to view a little more about this dancer's profile. I found a well thought-out, intriguing, and sincere statement of who he was and what his goals were in meeting a new dance partner. His profile read:

I am an active guy who likes to stay fit and explore new things. Being new to the area, I would like to share the exploration with someone who likes to stay active and maybe try some new things. Friends are very important to me and so that is where I would like to start, if it turns into more than that, all the better. That doesn't mean I have time for games, just that I think things are a lot more relaxed if you don't have too many expectations. Time with my daughter is important to me. Life through the eyes of a child—that has to excite you. I like a lady who is secure in her personal and professional life. What someone does is not as important as the passion put into it. A person who takes care of and respects herself is a real turn on. If you know who you are and have our own thoughts and opinions but have a little room to share it with others, I would love to hear from you. We will probably get along great. Bonus if you like a good glass of wine.

His ideal age range for a match was 32 to 47 years. After reading this, I found myself more intrigued by how I came to be listed as a potential partner. Clearly, I did not fit his specification, at least in terms of age. The nurturer in me began to take precedence. I would welcome being of assistance to this young man and helping him become acquainted with the area, so I responded with, "You are quite nice yourself."

And so this dance began.

First, we exchanged a few e-mails of a more informative nature about our backgrounds, occupations, and families. Then pleasantries turned into the exchange of telephone numbers. Once that happened, as I noticed with other dancers, the onscreen connection gave way to communication of a more personal nature. Hearing a person's voice and the manner in which he uses the English language outweighs all those written words in e-mails or texts. Online dating made me very aware of the senses' role in the art of communication. Listening to a new partner's voice, seeing him, and getting a sense of his body language and personal space were very important, and all affected my perception of the whole. Talking on the phone was the first true test of whether I would sense a like or dislike for another individual, on just a friendly level or possibly on a more intimate level. It was a process and an unpredictable one for sure. Mr. Waltz's voice was deep, with a sexy intonation, both deliberate and unforced in presentation. His words were slow and well thought out in conversation, never rushed. It was glorious to my discerning ear.

After many opportunities to speak, I wondered why we were interested in each other. With such an age difference and such geographical distance between us, not to mention the differences in where we were in our lives, why were we wasting each other's time? Being an overly cautious, independent, and financially secure woman, I had reservations about beginning and maintaining a potential long-term relationship with this young dance partner. Would I be just a safe haven from responsibility for him? Would our needs match or clash as we discovered the nuances and obstacles that accompany two individuals who are on completely different planes of life? Could this unlikely match fulfill my desire for long-awaited contentment and romantic happiness?

Skepticism prevailed at first. It was imperfect at best. My all-conservative thinking once again prevented my mind from allowing this dancer into the emotional corners of my life. However, we sensed a sensual or chemical attraction. How could I deny nature's voice calling through sexual pheromones?

No other dance partner even came close to creating these feelings in me.

The first connection began like the waltz—slow and calculating, a comfortable distancing between partners. After a casual exchange of pleasantries, I offered my services to steer him to new adventures in his new life. He was a young man and a father, the sole custodian of his 6-year-old daughter, and he needed guidance from a mother, one with daughters of her own. Choosing activities and places to go could be the bond that created our connection. I was ready to be the new family that was absent in this young man's life, a lifeline to a normal and vibrant community that he left behind.

Having lost both parents and a brother to cancer, he was alone and looking for a way to form a new kind of family. Without the nurturing of a mother and father and siblings that once enhanced his life, his quest to find someone to fulfill that void was paramount. I wondered if I was merely a conduit to help him fill that aspect of his life. Was that the only connection we would have? Was I willing to invest myself and my energies in someone who might only see me as a replacement for those whom he had lost? Would it be possible to become more than that? If he saw me as a mother figure, would we have the potential to become lovers or partners in intimacy? Why would a young and vibrant man in the prime of his life settle for a woman sixteen years his senior?

So the approach with this dancer would be one of friendship and guidance; I didn't expect more. I would be a wise figurehead, available for the needs of a young father. That was all. But how could we deny the chemistry, the ever-present desire to become closer in so many other avenues of a relationship? If I allowed myself to go to that ever-desirable place within my mind and possibly reveal too much to this dancer, would I ruin what platonic friendship we had already developed? The risk might outweigh the rewards of remaining just that, platonic friends. My musings and fantasies seemed to dominate my thoughts. Was I overthinking the possibilities and the past? The thought of pursuing a relationship only to be hurt and let down was painful. Why not enjoy the journey, as the cliché goes, and see what develops? Why not? Because I knew all too well in the depths of my soul what I wanted as an outcome. But would he want the same thing?

Our first meeting occurred late one night after a long day of work. I had only exchanged several messages with Mr. Waltz, and knew that he was exploring all that his new life and city had to offer. Had he experienced the excitement of the athletic events in the area? I would be the one to introduce him to his first Big Ten football game. Knowing that I was unable to attend an upcoming football game, I sent a brief text asking if he would like to find a friend and experience the event. Immediately he said yes, and we were to meet only so that I could give him the tickets. After agreeing on a convenient place to meet, I had very few expectations with regard to having a long conversation. I expected that we would just exchange a few pleasantries and be on our way.

Walking into the restaurant, I perused the bar area first, not really knowing who to look for. To my surprise, I spotted a man sitting very stoically at the bar. Sitting beside him was a little girl, a brown-eyed, black-haired child crumpled up in the chair, fighting to stay awake. I approached with a huge smile because this sight left me feeling immediately comfortable. Here was a very handsome and a quite stunning man, large in stature, tending gently to his little girl, rubbing her legs and gently stroking her hair. Wow, what a first impression. I do believe in the old saying about animals and children being the deal breakers or makers when it comes to creating a great first impression. Standing to greet me in a very gentlemanly fashion, Mr. Waltz pulled out the stool for me to sit. I decided that this was not a date, and in light of the fact that it was late and his daughter needed to get home to bed, I would merely exchange hellos and hand over the two tickets. To my surprise, Mr. Waltz insisted that I take a seat and enjoy a glass of wine with him.

I didn't want to appear ungrateful, so I accepted. The attraction had just begun. As I looked at this young man's face and body, I could see he was a lovely man in all superficial aspects. What was underneath this beautiful surface was what interested me. For now, I was the woman with the free tickets to a sporting event. The obligation he may have felt to buy me a drink and spend a few moments with me was merely that, and might have been the only reason for his consideration; we might never see each other after this night. I was resigned to that outcome, but my curiosity about him grew greater and greater as the conversation flowed. Here was a man of surprising intelligence and wisdom. Never had I sat with someone with whom it was so easy to carry on a conversation. He had an air of shyness about him, too.

So there I was, a mother figure responding to this man as if I were his tour guide. We proceeded with questions and answers regarding the little girl and all the wonderful opportunities that lay ahead for her in a large city like ours. I would assist him in any way he needed; after all, I was a mom to two daughters and had plenty of experience with all the ups and downs of raising girls. The way he showed his appreciation made me feel the happy fulfillment of helping someone once again. The evening ended with a quick hug with this commanding gentleman. It was a great feeling. Walking away to my car, all I could think was, oh, I hope he enjoys the game. Maybe I will see him again? At the very least, I knew he would contact me with a thanks for the tickets.

Two days went by and I was excited to receive a short text from Mr. Waltz. He was thrilled to have had the opportunity to go to the game, and was flattered that someone would think enough of someone she didn't really know to offer the tickets to him. This action set the tone for a potential relationship. I was happy to see that this man was considerate enough to thank me and so I responded with a "you're very welcome," and that I was happy to be able to provide him the opportunity, and that it was also a pleasure meeting him along with his lovely daughter.

The slow and calculating waltz continued from this moment on. Mr. Waltz continued to try to keep the lines of communication open, perhaps out of curiosity, or need for the nurturing that was so absent in his life now. Could I provide for him the secure family he so desired? Could I open the doors to a lifestyle he aspired to? I could create those connections. Being well aware of those possibilities would not prevent me from seeing how this all played out between us, even if we were two different individuals in different stages of life.

The next connection was initiated by Mr. Waltz.

"Hello, sunshine, I was wondering if you would allow me to take you to dinner?"

An offer for dinner in repayment for the tickets, perhaps? "Sunshine"? Was I his sunshine? Maybe he remembered the last line in my profile, "OPEN THE DOOR TO LET THE SUNSHINE IN"? The invitation was certainly unexpected but I accepted with delight.

We were to meet at a very lovely and quite exclusive restaurant. Not wanting to expose too much of my personal life, I decided that picking me up at my home was not an option quite yet. Knowing I must impress because he probably had dated a few very lovely young and beautiful woman, I felt a sense of competition. I always took pride in my appearance, but I put a little extra effort into appearing youthful as best I could by choosing the right clothes. Wearing a short black skirt, a tight-fitting leopard print sweater, and low-heeled boots, I felt comfortable in knowing I could match up to any woman twenty years younger. I suppose my confidence may have had an impact on Mr. Waltz because he appeared quite smitten that night, and his shy and demure manner indicated to me that he definitely was interested on a different level than I had expected from the start.

The dinner was delightful. Having met him at the door of the restaurant, I noticed a girlfriend sitting at the bar and proceeded to greet her. I discovered later that while we were chatting, my date talked to the waitress, requesting a booth that was a little more intimate. She commented on how refreshing and romantic this man was, to make sure we would have a bit of privacy during our night of dining.

Ah, and the night was long and lovely. A wine connoisseur, he examined particular wines from the list and inquired what type of food I planned to order so that he could suggest an appropriate wine to complement my meal. This was only the start of an evening during which a charming and extremely interesting man took the opportunity to create a dining experience that was more than inhaling food unnoticed. It was all about the quality of our experience, not merely filling our stomachs. He suggested hors d'oeuvres first, which were delightful. Recommending a taste of something I had never tried opened doors for me. I let him take the lead as in the waltz, knowing he would dance slowly and confidently, with class and ease. This was the dance of the evening. With each lifting of the fork or clinking of the wine glasses, we created memories that set the foundation for the rest of the dance. Another perusing of the wine list to choose another glass that would be best with our main meal extended the evening longer than I ever would have anticipated. I didn't want this dance to end. It was all so glorious and so sexy.

The evening continued with intense and in-depth conversation. It was all so interesting. The genuine and charming gentleman sitting across from me was a pleasant surprise. His long aquilinenose and masculine face gave way to a beautifully shaped balding, cleanly shaved head. His deep set and extremely intense blue eyes gazed my way with such intentness I couldn't help but imagine what was beyond the visual. Could I inch a little closer to open that door a little wider, letting the sun shine even brighter? I was hooked at this point, but was all too aware that my partner might be playing the game. I carefully examined his quiet and elegant demeanor with curiosity, thinking that this was probably the first scene in the first act in the dating stage of his life. Finding myself in a position of vulnerability at the hands of a man young enough to be my son was frightening. I put on my armor of emotional protection. This dancer would not destroy all the healing I had completed over the years. I would not become another actress on the stage to be tossed aside for someone more age appropriate down the road. Time to show control and restraint, and be careful not to allow this dance partner into a realm that was reserved for only those that desired more than a twirl around the stage with an anonymous partner. The evening ended with a brief hug and a thank you.

A week passed, and as I expected, I didn't hear from my waltz partner. I was somewhat relieved that I would not have to rehearse the dance with an uninterested partner.

The night was cold, and the parties of the holiday season were all a-bustle. A phone call with a surprise invitation to a business holiday gathering threw me off guard. It was my waltz partner.

"Hi. I would love to invite you over for a holiday drink."

I wondered if his other potential dates fell through. Why else would he want me to accompany him to a party where he would be seen with a woman who was not exactly age appropriate for him? As I examined my thoughts on how I should respond, I chose to keep my emotional wall up and declined the invitation. I sensed his extreme disappointment.

Moments later, another phone call came.

"I really want you to come over. Everyone wants to meet this lady I have been twirling on the dance floor."

It was tempting and certainly flattering, but I once again declined the invitation as it was late, and I was not dressed for such an occasion.

Reassuring me that I could come in sweats and look great, I knew he was serious about wanting me there. I accepted, and he agreed to meet me at the door in ten minutes. Quickly slipping into a casual, festive woolen skirt and a tight, three-quarter-length-sleeved black sheath top, I pulled up my messy hair into a bun and whipped on a pair of sparkly dangling earrings. Topped off with a pair of ankle-high black suede boots, I was ready to impress.

The very mature appearing gentleman who greeted me at the door set the wheels of emotional fantasy into play. My guard was let down, and now we could be seen as a playful duo with much to offer the group of mostly men. I became the center of the party.

Presenting me with a lovely glass of chardonnay, the night was young and the fun, carefree holiday party was a pleasant surprise. The waltz began again, but this time, I was ready to be swept off the dance floor into the arms of this unlikely partner. The night ended with another hug and expression of holiday cheer.

The number of phone calls after that night set the tone for a new and interesting relationship. Whatever that would be, I was determined to go along with this dancer. This partner would have to take the lead, and I would willingly follow as a good dance partner learns to do.

The days were filled with cooking and baking for the coming Christmas holiday. My family was home, and our plans were as always to enjoy Christmas Eve as a family. A phone call and an e-mail from my new dance partner wished me a Merry Christmas. That was an uplifting moment. I now felt the possibility that this dancer was really thinking of me as a possible partner too.

As the day went forward, thoughts of him were predominant in my mind. I felt compelled to invite this lonely man and his young daughter over for a holiday glass of wine, and or apple cider, along with the many holiday treats that were neatly arranged on a huge Christmas platter. Second guessing whether I should present this new young man to my family, I chose to ask them if it would be alright to invite a friend over for a short while. That all were in favor, which gave me a sense of relief and lifted this sense of obligation from my shoulders. I texted Mr. Waltz to see what his plans were. He typed back immediately.

> "We would love to come by. We were planning to see the holiday lights first so may we drop by later?"

"Of course, we would love to have you join in our holiday fun. Whatever works into your schedule."

With a great deal of gratitude, he entered my home with a bottle of very expensive dessert wine to complement the sweet treats. After the introductions, my family embraced his young daughter and proceeded to treat them both like family. Ah, this was certainly the moment that allowed for us to proceed with a different kind of relationship from the one we both initially expected. The night was joyous and filled with feelings of family, a feeling that I may have stimulated in his family too. As we conversed, I examined this man for clues if he was seeing his new dance partner as more than a friend. The eyebrows raised and the shy glances while turning away so as not to be revealed were so sweet, I could not help but to shower him with attention, much like a mother might comfort a child to create a safe environment. The quest was to make him feel totally comfortable in a situation that could have been quite the opposite. I accomplished that goal. The evening was a success.

The following day, I was greeted with texts of gratitude toward my entire family. He wrote that it was the first holiday in many years that had felt so special to him and his daughter. It was the greatest compliment of all! Along with that feeling came another underlying concern that, once again, I was providing the stable family environment that was missing in his life. Was that, and not romance, the draw to continue the dance? This question would be ever present for me in the coming weeks and months.

Our next date was attending a musical performance for children. It would be another opportunity to see if and how I would bond with his 6-year-old daughter, and if she would show interest in return. I approached this date with eyes wide open; I knew little girls. I knew all about their needs and wants and interests. This would be a piece of cake and fun at the same time. That day, I wore low-rise jeans and a cashmere turtleneck sweater. The show was delightful, and to watch the father-daughter dynamics would warm any mother's heart. I kept my distance, not wanting to appear too eager to replace a birth mother who was only occasionally present.

After the show, we decided to shop at a local mall for little girls' clothes. He showed good taste in what he wanted for his daughter—classy and smart, yet trendy clothes. Once again, this indicated to me that he wanted a more classy lifestyle. He knew what he wanted for her, and to me, that was a definite turn-on.

As we rode the elevator, my new dancer asked me a strange question, after telling me that tall men love tall women.

"What kind of boots would you wear? I am going to buy you a pair of cowboy boots one day."

Aghh! What was I to think at this moment? Yes, there were a few sexual undertones that played along with this comment—at least I felt so. I let the comment go and did not respond. The reference to sexy boots suggested that he had sexual intentions, which I was not quite ready for.

The end of the day included a cupcake treat at a local bakery and visit with Santa, all innocent and nonthreatening. It was delightful. I discovered that I loved being around young children and savored the moments with his 6-year-old as if I were reliving all those glorious moments with my own daughters at that age. Maybe this was what I was meant to do. I now looked forward to other future meetings together as a family. Could that be possible? I could dream it, but was that realistic? Those damn boots.

Adapting to many different venues was a gift this young man had acquired. The following weekend, it was my turn to invite him to a formal dinner at an exclusive club. Would he accept, and would he be able to feel comfortable in a new situation with people whom he did not know? He accepted with great enthusiasm. Those questions were answered very quickly. Introductions to a number of my acquaintances allowed me to observe the level of comfort this gentleman felt in this new situation. The evening was a success.

As the dance continued, we found ourselves wanting to spend any available time together, no matter what the circumstances. During the week, dinner was always a must. Casual or elegant, we seemed to find time for one another. The waltz became more fluid now. Every step was not calculating nor carefully thought out. We felt freedom to flow with one another along the avenues of life. It all seemed so comfortable, albeit still platonic. There were hints of sexual tension from both of us, never discussed but always implied. That to me kept the intrigue and thrill lasting longer than it would have if we had already consummated a relationship without really knowing the other person on a more in-depth level. If there was one thing that I had learned by selecting those dancers on my card, it was to slowly, and with wisdom, give in to animalistic needs. Moving too quickly would only succeed in ending that union faster than the speed of light. The mystery would be over, and the connection would only be superficial.

We continued to practice on this simple level for some time. We discovered each other's athleticism when we decided to pack up our ski gear and take a trip north to the snowy hills of Northern Wisconsin. I knew that I was capable of handling myself, but was this another test to see if we were compatible in that aspect of a relationship?

That day I saw a man who was clearly a natural athlete, and to watch him maneuver the hills like a professional was a complete turn-on. Swooshing down the slick frozen slopes, all the while assisting me in my less-than-perfect skills showed him to be a compassionate, concerned partner. He was a talented, physical specimen for sure, adding another element of attraction. At this moment, the slow and fluid waltz would move into a whole new level of twirls and spins. I knew that we both were waiting for the other to make some sort of intimate move. He was too shy and guarded to think that I would be interested. I felt precisely the same way. How did we approach the situation? We played it as it came.

The moonlit night encompassed the sky after the day of exhausting and bone-chilling exercise, allowing for his 6-year-old daughter's early bedtime. When she was tucked in bed after a nighttime story, we were alone. Two glasses of pinot grigio emerged, and we gazed into one another's eyes, setting off a flurry of unexpected emotions. As he gently took my glass to place it on the counter, seductively focusing on my eyes, he slipped his big and muscular arms around my waist, drawing me close to his large frame. Never breaking the glance, pulling me into his chest and, swaying back and forth to the music playing, he gently danced with me, the seductive, mutual motion of two bodies united as one. With his free hand, he gently caressed my cheekbones with his thumb, smiling like a teenager about to romantically sweep his young girlfriend off the dance floor and into the safe haven of his warm and inviting bedroom.

Oh what a rush! I was that young teenage girl again. How was it possible to feel this way again after so many years of mediocrity? Go with the flow, I reminded my organized mind. Enjoy the moment, as I have told so many over the years. The process is sometimes better than the end product. I will never say that again. With this man, the entire dance was more than superb. The moves, step by step along this floor of excitement, would culminate in nothing short of a standing ovation. Two standing ovations.

Breathless, he pulled my face toward his, and in a sweet move, pressed his beautiful lips to mine; with each short and tender touch, our lives became united. We were one. The mystery of the what ifs or would it happen was now at my fingertips. I was living the excitement of a first kiss, one that I have never forgotten. He continued to take the initiative as all our protective armor was dissolved into thin air. The excitement escalated to a passionate exchange of more expressive kissing. Introducing the sweet smell of breath, his tongue entered my mouth. The swirling of that soft, sweet tasting tongue made me feel as if we were circling the dance floor. Our tongues explored the depths of the moist and velvety corners of our mouths. It was all too sensual. I didn't want this to end, and it didn't. It was the prelude to many hours of exploration on a completely different level than we ever would have expected.

Finally, I knew he did find me attractive, and I certainly felt similarly. Taking my small hand into his large hand, he led me to his lower level. He strategically slipped my sweater over my head and carefully ran his finger down my long slender neck to the midpoint of my breasts. I felt the erectness of my nipples. With little trepidation, he placed his hand under and around my right breast while slowly moving his body downward, placing his mouth around my left breast while he stroked my right nipple. The erotic and gentle nature of his touch comforted me; I knew what was to come. My mind was saying, how could this be? My body was following his slow and rhythmic and synchronized movements. Much like the leader of a waltz, he was guiding me through each move. We were holding hands through the slow pace of this elegant and methodical dance. In this simple dance form, one just has to sway with the other's body in accordance with the tempo of the music, and in this instance, the beat of our trembling bodies. Being slow, it didn't take much effort to adjust to the beats and dance accordingly. In a waltz, the leader guides his partner by pushing and pulling the partner. Both should be in sync with each other, swaying back and forth and sideways effortlessly, without any awkwardness. It is a beautiful form of art. We were moving across the dance floor of intimacy; the canvas was us, the artists, showcasing our Impressionist brushstrokes on this dance of love. The movements required both of us to follow a certain tempo, in perfect coordination with each other. We, the dancers, had to connect with our minds and touch to understand and coordinate, to prepare for the next step or to move, providing a perfect balance.

It is said that ballroom dancing and romance go hand in hand, as couples are perfecting their moves on the dance floor and in life. This night was one of grace and rhythm, and much as ballroom dancing has a romantic aura around it, so did this evening with a man who proved to have such correct posture and a sophisticated personality. This dance fit him perfectly.

He laid me slowly onto his bed made up with gray flannel sheets, and tucked the soft and aromatic pillow under my head, all the while gazing into my eyes. We never stopped to look away. Eliciting a brief and curious smile from me, he quietly responded, "There is that beautiful smile.

"You make me shiver all over. You are like sunshine," he said.

As his words flowed sensually, I couldn't help but think that this man was mature beyond his years. He was genuine, loving, and extremely romantic, not the shy and quiet man I first met at that bar so many months ago. He transformed into a seductive leading actor from a 1920s classic movie.

Gently stroking my inner thighs with those large and enveloping hands, he strategically swished his palm over my pubic area, teasing my loins, raising the sexual tension to a point of extreme stimulation. This was my cue to begin the slow caressing of a body that was fit, firm, and very masculine. My hands began to explore his massive broad and hairy chest while exploring the undulations of musculature that seemed to ripple like the waves of the ocean. I could sense a vulnerability that allowed me to begin to lead in the dance of love. I wanted to savor every delicious moment and caress him, so with deliberate and slow strokes, I began pressing his head down to mine. It was a tender moment for both of us. Having long, aquiline German noses, it was comfortable pressing up against each other. The fit was perfect. I worked ever so slowly to the nape of his neck, massaging the indentations of his sternum and chest, while I was anticipating where the next area of study might be. The tense trapezius muscle just below his upper neck extending down to the scapular indents in his back lent itself to a long and forceful gliding stroke up and down his spinal column. As I released the inner tension, this man became putty in my firm yet gentle hands. What a glorious controlling sensation. I now was in charge of what lay ahead, and he opened his body and soul to allow me in. The flood of sexual emotions flowed through our conjoined bodies. We were one. A fluid coordination of bodily movements, the dance of intimacy had begun.

Creating a sense of calm was important to the exploration of the other half of this magnificent, masculine human specimen. Pressing our bodies tightly, a vacuum formed, and the dew from his broad and glorious chest accumulated on the coarse and plentiful dark hair extending all the way to his soft pubic mound. Erotic as it may have felt, the sweet and gentle nature we each brought to this encounter was more than an unrequited sexual act, much more than that. I gently slid my long fingers along the head of his totally erect penis. I examined the length tactilely, working my middle three fingers along a shaft that seemed endless. The virility of this man would never be in question. As I fondled the circumference, the rush of pulsating blood forced its way along the elongated shaft. Stimulated by this reaction, I found myself feeling as I did 30 years before, as a young and naïve girl experiencing her first sexual and romantic encounter.

Preparing naturally for the inevitable, the pure, unadulterated excitement was indescribable. The loving and throbbing manhood would soon be exploring areas that were saved for only the special few that came into my life. He was one of the few. Stroking him at the same time as I placed the tip of the circumcised head in between my legs, I could feel a sense of urgency and exhilaration coming from him. He wanted to feel the warm and soft inner sanctuary between my thighs. Was I ready for this?

I let nature guide my blurred senses. He slowly slipped the top of his throbbing penis into the wet and warm orifice of my vagina. He was careful to make sure that I was comfortable, a few words were exchanged, and I assured him it was oh-so-fine and please proceed. Inserting the shaft stimulated an electrical impulse in my vaginal wall, the like of which I had never felt before. Moving slowly in and out, the pulsating continued with increased force. To feel the grand organ entering into my ever-so-ready body was more than exhilarating. As each forward thrust and then backward movement increased the flow of vaginal juices, I realized the probability that this man could control all physical urges to release and provide satisfaction for me as his partner.

The marathon of love would last for what seemed like hours. Stimulating the very core of my being, I moaned with sheer pleasure with every exaggerated thrust. The pleasure was unmatched by anything that I had ever known. I only hoped that I was able to reciprocate by giving such feelings of pleasure to this man who lay heavily on top of me. His passion continued. He experimented with a new position; pulling my legs high into the air and over his shoulders, he reentered, kneeling beside my perpendicular body. Grabbing tightly to my long and muscular calves, the push and pull of the dance would culminate in a robust and mind-altering move. To observe the raw and sensual sexual pleasure etched in the face of this commanding person gave me such a feeling of joy and relief, relief that I was able to excite and stimulate this young man to such levels. That had been my question and fulfillment was reached for both. A genuine and loving smile emerged from this man who loved my aging and exhausted body. Dropping to my side, he flipped my body to his right side and pulled me close to his front to embrace lovingly. That embrace created a lasting moment better than any ejaculatory response. This was the reason for all the precursors, the actual loving of two bodies and souls. A closeness would develop for us far beyond that of two separate individuals seeking only a platonic relationship. Everything would change now, I felt. Or would it?

Slowly slipping out of bed, Mr. Waltz found a soft black and velvety robe for me to slip into. He would do the same. We opened the sliding glass door on this snowy and chilly night, glasses of wine in hand. He placed his hand on the back of my robe and let it slowly slide down my back. I stepped into a hot and steamy tub for more passion. The mist evaporating in the cold air instantly formed translucent crystals in the air. Strategically situating out bodies close to one another, we raised our glasses to the moonlit sky and embraced for what would be a long and romantic few hours. The stars were glistening and the moon dimly lit this man who did not take his eyes off of me. With such deep and piercing eyes, he was enjoying all that this night had offered. I was savoring each moment as well and did not want it to end.

"You are beautiful in the moonlight. Why am I so lucky?" he asked.

"Why am *I* so lucky?" I replied.

"Your former husband must be nuts."

It was a moment of affirmation. I could be adored and cherished. For the first time in six years, here was a man who saw all that I had to offer and was appreciative that he could be on the receiving end. I was totally caught off guard and did not know how to respond, but something in me gave me the strength to say, "I know, you are right." I was confident in knowing that I could provide and did offer much more than many other women out there. If and only if he was ready to accept it, this overall confidence presented to him the turn-on that he was looking for in a partner on or off the dance floor.

Is there a shelf life for love and passion? I would soon discover those romantic and desirous lustful feelings would last much longer than anticipated. Previous relationships seemed to blossom rapidly and, without notice, abruptly disappear along with the setting sun. Our sun was shining. I was his sunshine.

It was all so confusing. As I reflected on my life after my marriage, I wondered how can two people with similar loves and desires fall into a long and comfortable passion that both want desperately, only to have it fade without warning? Yes, there must be a shelf life or a certain amount of time allotted for love when the chemistry of two people is so potent in the beginning and then its effectiveness wears thin. But what then? Does one decide to move on to the next pursuit in hopes of continuing that thrill of chemical excitement for another few months or years? What about the next time? Should a relationship end at the point when both people get too comfortable and the thrill of newness and wonderment are no longer present? Scientifically speaking, the chemical attraction between two people begins with a thrust of thrill and excitement for the first 4 to 13 months and then wanes, along with the interest in one another.

Any relationship must involve more than just the sexual thrill of enjoying each other's bodies. The key to a lasting and meaningful relationship involves a great deal more than the mere chemistry of the body. It must incorporate the mind, and all the varying interests each can bring to a mutually satisfying union, one that encourages learning, discovering the other's innermost desires and interests in life, and helping to nourish and fulfill a lifetime of exploration together.

In our new relationship, the weeks and months seemed to pass quickly with exciting and stimulating conversation during dates and in the bedroom. Unfortunately, there continued to be an emotional distancing by both parties for fear of being rejected. I wondered if he really wanted more from me in this relationship, or if I was merely the conduit for his personal growth on a social level as well as fulfilling his sexual needs. Possibly, I would tell myself. Should I bring up the subject with the knowledge that the conversation could end what we had going right now, all the while revealing what my true desires were, or should I let sleeping dogs lie? Being the emotional individual that I am, I felt the need to approach the subject in a delicate but safe way. His answer would always be, "I will never hurt you. I have not found anything about you that I do not like, and we enjoy so many things together. I love your company. You are the sunshine of my life."

With the cautious, hardened shell that I carry, I would always reassure him that I was content in where my life was and did not want it to change. Knowing very well that there was a chance that I could really fall into a deep and loving emotional commitment with this man, a feeling I would only reserve for a select few, I would not allow him to get beyond my superficial shell. I would stay in control, and let the chips fall where they may.

The next few outings continued the exciting moments filled with energy and intimacy. Downhill skiing, skating, sledding, tennis, dancing, dinners, balls, sporting events, quiet dinners alone, hot tubbing, trips to Chicago, and motorcycle trips to wine country were some of the activities we enjoyed together. The stars were aligned along with our personalities. There were so many similar traits between the two of us that I often wondered if they might tend to turn our relationship stale. When both people are too much alike, those similarities may not offer a couple the opportunity to explore different perspectives or enough energy to enlighten them and strengthen their relationship. But for us there did not seem to be a dull moment. Conversations flowed, and mutual interest and comfortable moments were plentiful.

Our contacts with one another went on throughout the week, though we saw each other much less frequently than a typical monogamous couple would have. Generally, it was limited to a call midweek about what each other's plans were for the week and if dinner would be included in that. Sometimes we planned a ski trip or tennis on the weekend after he dropped his daughter off at her mother's. The feeling of commitment was there, and the thought that there may be other women in his life diminished with each passing week only because he just didn't have the time to invest in more than one woman along with his work and childcare commitments. This was the only reassuring feeling I had that maybe I was the only one he was truly interested in. While we dated, I continued to keep my options open by communicating with other dance partners in cyberspace, but never in-depth and never with guilt. I was just realistic in knowing that this one person who was showing me so much attention could move on after he had used me for whatever it was he needed at the present time.

Someone once told me that certain people come into our lives for a very special reason, and they are there to fulfill a present need. So cherish the time together, and if something develops, it is meant to be, but if not, look at it as a stepping stone to the next person who enters into your life and prepare yourself for another interesting ride.

Maybe I was that stepping stone for Mr. Waltz! This is what was always in the back of my mind now. One false belief that it is important to let go of is the belief that we need another person in our lives to make us whole. "As long as we believe that someone else has the power to make us happy, we are setting ourselves up to be victims," as explained in *Codependence: The Dance of Wounded Souls*, by Robert Burney.

One cold January evening we planned on attending an exquisite social event within the community, one where the who's who of the community attended, called The Frostiball. I would once again create an unlikely opportunity to experience an event for my dance partner. It was an elegant affair of champagne drinking, dancing, and romance. For my dance partner, it was also another introduction into an unfamiliar world. A lovely elegant dinner before the event was the precursor to an evening of sheer ecstatic, emotional connection between two individuals who were in need of love and tenderness. Filling the tall, fluted glasses with the rose colored sweet and aromatic champagne created uninhibited moments. Looking deeply into each other's eyes while dancing closely to the rhythm of the music echoing through this large mystical room, filled with people from all walks of life, we entered into a venue of fun and many introductions.

Flowing gently across the dance floor, my black crepe draped gown with an open back exposed the lower and most intimate area of my lumbar spine, which was adorned with diamond-like bling-bling. I felt like Cinderella at the ball. Sweeping the floor gently with elegant, fluid motions, we were the only ones on the dance floor at that moment. With our hearts filled with excitement and heads filled with wine, we were free to be and to explore the ever-present possibilities of showing affection in a public venue. We were too engrossed in each other to care what others would think or say the next morning. Mr. Waltz lifted me up by placing his hands under my arms, and we began twirling and twirling around center stage. The centrifugal force created vertigo in my already spinning head. His strength carrying my limp body for that period of time only confirmed to me that he really had the hots for me, and did not want to let go for fear someone else would take over. The tumultuous dance became even more erotic as the night progressed. We gazed deeply into each other's eyes while we flirted on the wooden dance floor. The intoxicating beverages were not the only things that filled our empty minds with excitement; uninhibited moments of joys and exhilaration did as well. This was clearly the beginning of the dance of love and lust—two human beings coming together as one.

The night was still and the mood changed from exuberance and energetic elation to the softer, more solemn moments as we pulled ourselves away from the crowd. This would be a memorable dance of the night, one that was only in its beginning stages. Anticipation of what was to come made for an even greater sense of thrill. I wanted to be swept off that dance floor into an environment that only two loving and somewhat shy individuals would share alone.

The home was empty—no children, no dogs or other distractions to allow the mood to escape. We were both free of the constraints of everyday life. Free to explore once again the forbidden avenues of love. The amorous steps were set in motion. To be held and be embraced by this masculine and yet tender man was the beginning of a loving and titillating night of lovemaking that would last for hours. For the first time in my life, I did not have that feeling of being bored and wanting to end the sexual act. This was more than that. It was true, unadulterated lovemaking by two individuals who respected and cared for each other, who admired and truly had a chemical connection with each other. What a joyous and surprising outcome to a dazzling night.

The morning came all too soon, and my partner was out the door to return to the normal activities of life, but before leaving, he gave me another reassuring and tender embrace, which was meaningful and loving.

"Good morning, sunshine. How do you do it? Looking as beautiful in the morning as you did last night?"

He clearly adored his newly found dance partner and wanted to return to the floor for an encore. This would have to wait until the next time we would meet.

From that day forward, we were inseparable. Continuing with this new partner was frightening and yet fulfilling. I was always wondering when it would end. With some partners, there is always that concern, but in my current stage of life, I was so content with what life offers. The willingness and ability to move in many other directions without fear and anxiety of loss had been eliminated from my consciousness, partially because I had become immune and desensitized to those feelings of dependency or codependency. The addiction to that drug had been eliminated through years of detoxification. The chemicals needed for desire had diminished, and thus, contentment and self-satisfaction were prominent emotions in my life. Expectations were few, allowing for complete freedom to express myself truthfully within the confines of a newly developed relationship. This freedom only allowed two partners to be more open with one another without the fear of wondering what might happen.

What was the next step? Should we complete this dance and begin a new series of dances to see if the compatibility on and off the dance floor would continue? Or should we continue to practice to make sure that we were in line with each step, growing a strong and mutually agreeable partnership? Time was in our favor. Waltzing into the sunset could be in the cards for this unlikely and once-apprehensive couple. I was his sunshine, and he was my light.

From the moment of our first glance and then touch on this dance floor, we began the ultimate of romantic moves that would carry us into a long-lasting love affair, a love affair on the dance floor. The deep and soulfully intense feeling of someone looking right through to my soul was scary, to be sure, but exhilarating as well. When he was taking my hands in his own, his gentle way of unfolding each finger to entwine with the others and then pulling me close to his broad, tight, and physically fit chest made my heartbeat increase, an arrhythmia that took my breath away. Placing my head on his chest, the pounding of his echoing heart was evident, and our movements became one. Never pushing and pulling one another, always connected, he held me close and never distanced himself from me. I was now his partner, his sunshine.

My need or desire for this man to be close was apparent, and he would continually lace his long arms around my waist, forcing me to take in deep breaths, tightening those side and stomach muscles. Conscious of the age and body difference, I had to remind myself that I was beautiful and deserving of this man. Unfortunately, this would be an ongoing insecurity for me. Never before had I felt the pressure or the need to be the best, if not better, than those around me. The competition was far too great and ever present. Fortunately, he was not at all concerned about the insignificant insecurities I was feeling. He saw me as a classic beauty, a woman who knew who she was and where she was going, with all the passion and zest for life that he desired. Could it be that he was a bit intimidated by this very successful and talented woman? A challenge? Someone he had always longed for, but never encountered until now? A substitute mother perhaps?

The dance of wonder began. Would I ever let those cautious notions dissipate, and would he ever reveal his true desire to be with me? Fear of the possibility of rejection from one another created an undercurrent that would continue until one day we would confront it head on. For now, it was sufficient to continue the satisfying and exciting relationship. Neither wanted to ruin what was positive for now.

As the months passed, so did the question of where this relationship would be going, as the slow and melodic and uncalculating connection became stronger and stronger with each experience. There were no long-term expectations from either side, though there were questions concerning thoughts of a long-term, fulfilling love match. These questions were not answered; the implications were certainly there, but knowing how these things usually pan out, unrealistic expectations were never part of the equation. So the dance continued, and the enjoyment of each other's company was superb.

People said that we were male and female counterparts because of our very similar temperaments, values, ideas, thoughts, and desires. It was like looking into a mirror, only one that showed the opposite gender. The kind, compassionate, caring young man possessed a soul of wisdom and sensibility. His was an old soul, more than many other older men's. His gentleness and sensitivity to mankind and animals was ever present. The ability to command respect from animals, as well as a sense of love, came so naturally to him. He was a dog whisperer of sorts, like Cesar Milan. He frequently helped me care for and train my dog; his interest in helping me manage this part of my life was endearing. Offers to care for my pets while I was traveling only emphasized his desire to become a bigger part of my life. This became a pattern over the months that followed.

With the increased interest in my favorite exploits, Mr. Waltz put forth an inordinate amount of effort to become involved in activities that were important to me. He immersed himself in learning with pleasure the game of tennis, joining leagues, lessons, and drills. A very talented and natural athlete, he was more than capable of keeping up with me and loved every minute of it. The athletic prowess of this young man was invigorating to me, and also an extreme turn on. Being an athlete myself, it was a priority for me to find someone equally interested in athletics, and Mr. Waltz was.

We planned a trip south—beaches, tennis, golf, and a trip to Disney World with his 6-year-old daughter, which proved to be the highlight of our ongoing relationship. Always cautious about being with someone for the first time for any extended period of time, I felt this would be a test of compatibility. I was wary about a new person invading my private space and being able to tolerate it, let alone enjoy it, but the latter proved to be the case, much to my surprise. Every waking moment was filled with joy and anticipation of more exciting times together as a unit. Conflict was not present nor was tension, only curiosity and excitement.

The first time issues developed regarding allowing his daughter to experience the closeness between her father and a woman who was not her mother was when we had to decide where everyone would sleep in small quarters during this trip. It became clear that she needed to be aware that I was more than just a friend who daddy was spending time with. The visual and intimate moments we shared—a kiss, a long embrace—would be part of her life now, and she needed to be comfortable with this, and know that it was a natural progression when a man and a woman care for one another. He was clear about making this an important factor in her emotional growth. This was normal, and she needed to allow another person in her life.

The progression continued slowly and carefully. The immature thinking of a 6-year-old had to be approached with care. She accepted my presence, but also felt a sense of competition for her daddy's attention. So many moments were interrupted so we could attend to the little girl's needs. Combining already existing families and their histories became an important and prominent part of our developing relationship; incorporating others who had little or no connection to our respective pasts was a new adventure.

The days, weeks, and months that followed revolved around a new concept of family. We started to develop new memories and history, to be shared in the future with a completely new set of dance partners Our specific habits, quirks, and patterns emerged in a clearer light. At first we were oblivious to all of these maybe trivial idiosyncrasies; but as our partnership developed beyond that which was strictly chemical and sexual, we were better able to see the little things that made us up as individuals. These discoveries were not always what we were hoping for.

I wondered, can I adjust to the change? Change is always happening in all of us, but subtly so, and this new relationship brought bigger changes. Imagine having a greater portion of your life consumed by someone other than who you are with at present. Imagine learning to adapt to a new personality and style, new interests, looks, mannerisms, even the way of driving a car. Imagine how much there would be to learn: what foods the new partner likes, whether he sleeps on the left or right side of the bed, snores, goes naked, has restless leg syndrome, is an early riser, or a late night partier or a drinker. Would he be a conversationalist? Insecure? An extrovert or an introvert? Would he have high energy or low energy? Would he be athletic? How would you learn about your shared interests, his commitment issues, or his history when dealing with relationship problems? Would he be aggressive, complacent, kind, introspective, calm, communicative? I had to answer all these questions as we navigated our new relationship, dealing with real changes on a day-to-day basis. Whether good or bad, changes were inevitable, and each partner in this dance needed to become aware of and adjust to them in order to create a harmonious living environment.

Moments of discord begin to surface as the months moved forward. The somewhat uncomfortable gatherings with respective family members, all of whom were learning to adapt and adjust to new people in the household could be tense at first, only because the initial thrill of first meeting that dance partner on the floor was over now. The reality of learning the difficult steps to move forward comfortably and successfully in this dance were less fluid and exciting. It became a little more like work, as both parties were on guard for fear of failing to correctly make that next important step or move in the relationship.

That first summer was wonderful. With plentiful summer activities that we both enjoyed together as a couple, along with the warm sultry nights to carry the day into evenings, we carried on effortlessly with a confidence and joy that surprised the skeptics even closest to them. Days spent on the lake boating, water-skiing, swimming; playing tennis, biking, hiking—these activities certainly lent themselves to creating days of pleasure and togetherness. As the relationship became more comfortable and went on, I anticipated that the electrical stimulation would short out. Quite the opposite occurred. The intimate moments were many, and the anticipation and desire seemed to increase. Every intimate act became a new and exciting exploration of infinite possibilities. We were vulnerable and wide open, allowing for experimentation. These pleasurable moments were enough to stimulate even the biggest of contrarians.

Whew! If only every man and woman could have such pleasure at least once in their lives. This was certainly my first, but was this chemistry the factor that should bind two individuals? Was all this too good to be true? Would issues surface and make these dance partners stumble and try to regain their footing to carry on? These were the continued questions in the back of my mind that were hidden, ever present, but never spoken of. I kept coming back for more, despite my questions and the possibility of upcoming obstacles. The obstacles were greater than even I expected.

It was a warm and sultry, humid summer evening, almost a year to the day since we met. After dinner and glass of wine at my home, a somber and quite nervous Mr. Waltz needed to reveal something so important to him; he prepared me gently for a conversation I was not ready for.

"I have to tell you something, and I am sorry for waiting this long, but I knew there would never be a right time."

Seeing the fear and trepidation in his eyes, he sat me down and knelt beside my chair. I was confused and said, "Are you sick?" Knowing that his brother had died of lung cancer at a very early age, I supposed there was a genetic predisposition to this cancer, and asked if he was hiding his illness from me. No, that was not it. With great difficulty he began to say, "I know this may be the last time you want to see me after telling you this fact about my life, but you need to know in order for me to move forward with *us*. I have to tell you if there will be a future between us. I am prepared to say I have spent the best year of my life with you and will relish this, and am grateful for having this special dance with such an incredible, loving, caring, and thoughtful woman as yourself. I am blessed. So here goes.

"When I was old enough to be able to understand, I was told by my dying brother that I was adopted. The age difference between my brother and myself was quite great, but I never thought too much about it. A bonus baby perhaps? Being a grown adult now, and the only son to be left to parents who were witnessing the slow and agonizing last breaths of their oldest and golden child, it was paramount to him that I be told the truth, regardless of how hurtful and damaging it might be.

"I had been brought home from an orphanage from upstate New York and was adopted at the age of one year."

Throughout the years, there seemed to be conflict and emotional distance between this new baby boy and his now new siblings, a brother who was an accomplished athlete and went on to become the dean of a college, and a sister 16 years his senior who, at best, merely acknowledged this new person in their family. The dynamics in this one-time family of four changed. The lack of a brotherly or sisterly bond was hurtful, and because he grew up with parents who would be considered elderly, and because he had much older siblings, he was a more mature child, different from other boys his age. He was spoiled and maybe overly protected in too many areas of his life. This protectiveness proved to be a detrimental thing for him.

The hard fact was, he was lied to. Accepting this fact was difficult at first, but then his interest in finding out who he really was and where he came from became more important. Who were his real parents? After a lot of searching and after the death of his father, the truth was accidentally revealed. His father and brother were dead; only his sister, 16 years his senior, and his mother remained as his family, and his mother was dependent on him as her only family member; his sister was not close to them.

With shock and extreme grief, the truth of who his biological mother was became clear.

"At the age of 16, my sister had gotten pregnant. She was sent away to have the baby to give it up for adoption. After my birth, I was placed in an orphanage for an entire year. With regret, my parents, who were actually my grandparents, set out to adopt me, their grandson, to be raised in the only family I have ever known. From then on, my biological mother, who everyone claimed was my sister, had little or no use for the baby she gave birth to."

What a revelation. I felt very sorry for this dance partner for what he had to go through—the many years of dealing with this lie had been difficult, and his sadness was apparent. He had a sister, who was really his mother, and who wanted nothing to do with him. For all practical purposes, he was nonexistent to her.

"Over the years, my mother—my sister—married and had three other sons, all of whom are near my age and would be my half-brothers. There has been very little contact between these family members, but not for lack of trying on my part."

He was alone now and his family included only his little girl.

My sympathy for this man after this personal and painful information was revealed was enormous. What a way to tear at a person's heartstrings. It certainly did mine. It was not an issue to anyone but him, and even now, it was the past and he had moved forward in creating a new family. I was exhausted emotionally for Mr. Waltz. I needed to find my bearings and comfort him in his time of need. But this night proved to have been just getting started with all those underlying demons that we never want exposed.

So this was the precursor that led to the next important revelation about this most mysterious man. What could top this? Was I prepared for more personal details from this man's past life? The room became all too quiet after I digested the first bit of information, and the need to reflect and process was done.

Trembling, he was ready to share the extremely personal information about who he was, and what other secrets he had held onto tightly. Kneeling by my side, this large-framed man immediately reverted to the appearance of a young, innocent, and helpless boy, one who needed approval from those who were important to him now in his life. But in order to do that, he had to open up about all of his imperfections. This was a big one.

"Back when I was fresh out of college, I met a young woman at a bar. I was 21-years-old, and had a great job with a big company. We entered into an intimate relationship, which lasted for a few months. I came to know her mother, who was inseparable from her daughter. The mother-daughter duo would frequent the bars to pick up men. I didn't know that this girl was underage. She told me she was 19. This girl shunned the other men that she had been with, and when they found out I was her next love interest, they exposed the fact that she was only 16, and the next thing I knew, the cops were at my door. I was arrested and charged with inappropriate acts with a minor, third degree sexual assault. I was prosecuted for statutory rape, which the courts define as having sex with anyone under the age of 16.

"The police were tipped off by a person who once dated her and was cast off. He was angry at her and at me, the new love in her life, and in retaliation he called the police. I was the one to feel the repercussions of his frustration.

"It was a time in my life I would like to forget, an awful and terrifying time in my life. The court gave me a year in prison. After that my entire life changed. Life as a convict was indescribable, and there were many moments when I didn't know if I would survive. Later, I attempted to get the courts to overturn the conviction, but the courts kept the ruling. I had discovered that the mother-daughter duo had played this game with others, and I was one of their victims. That doesn't dismiss the plain and simple fact that I broke a law. I am responsible for the fact that I was with a minor and I paid the price for it, not only for a year, but for the rest of my life. I have to register anywhere I go. If I'm unemployed or interviewing for a job, or trying to get a loan, the question is there right on the form: Have you ever been convicted of a crime?

"This will haunt me forever. I am not a criminal or a bad person. There are bad people out there, and I am very cautious about who I let into my life and share things with. You can understand this. I did not approach the subject because felt that you needed time to really get to know who I am as a person before you knew me as the branded individual, this shame I have to live with. I have a professional degree and owned my own business, only to fold it all up and move away from the area. I was ostracized from a community that I called home. I was an embarrassment to my family, though all of the people who really knew me supported me from the beginning and saw the rightful end of what was tragically a wrongdoing. Now I am here, and have surrounded myself with good people who can only be positive influences in my life and on my daughter. You have been that in so many ways, and I thank you from the bottom of my heart for that. I can understand your hesitation to want to see me anymore. That is why I needed to tell you and allow you to know me in my entirety. No questions, no secrets. I am exposed literally and figuratively and am willing to expose more if need be."

Silence. Oh my God, how could I process all this incredible information in one sitting? My initial reaction was one of fear. What else was this man hiding? So many of us have hidden pasts and agendas that we would rather not share. But this one was a doozy. Having my own insecurities about my age and my status and what his ulterior motives were, I felt this information only exacerbated those insecurities and fears. All I could do was first feel hurt and confused and slightly sorry for this man kneeling in front of me with tears in his eyes. Was I a dupe or was I one to look at the entire picture and forgive?

My other, more pervasive thoughts were about his incarceration. What was it like for a convicted rapist? What other kinds of criminals were residing there? Did he have a cellmate? Who could one befriend in that sort of environment? But the biggest question in my perverse mind at this point was, was he somebody's *bitch*? Was it true that men in prison look to other men for sexual gratification? I didn't want to go there, but I was worried. I had been intimate with someone who might have been with another man or, even worse, other men, which could mean I was at risk for some sexually transmitted disease, even a life threatening one. I was mad, confused, and afraid. I didn't even want to go there. I never asked the question. It was disgusting to think about, and it also opened up a dialogue about sexually transmitted diseases. This was always a concern festering in the corner of my now-fragile mind. With a moment to rest my now-confused mind, I was at a loss to respond. Frankly, I wanted him to leave, allowing me to collect my thoughts before I responded. I knew I needed to be tested, as did he.

Instead I said, "I remember when I was 15, even 14, and how sexual a girl is at that age, and naïve. One doesn't consider the ramifications of legality when the hormones are flowing and two parties are engaged in what may be a first or newly discovered exciting moment involving something so natural as sexual activity."

I did not fault him for that, curiously enough. What I was more concerned about was that he kept this part of his past hidden, even during our open conversations. Understandably so, but still. What other surprises did he have in store for me? Should I be tested for a disease? Was I being used and manipulated? And once again I wondered, since there was such an age difference, why would he be interested in me in the first place? Was it the need for a family, a mother figure to carry on the duties as a mother to his daughter? I was the same age as his real biological mother and that was freaky.

Did he see a cash cow in front of him, one who could provide that lifestyle for him and his only family, a lifestyle that, after hearing all of this, I knew he aspired to now? I need time to decipher all that he had put in front of me.

"This may take a while," I said.

Mr. Waltz exited with head down.

The days went on, and we did not contact each other, but I felt such guilt and sorrow for his plight and all that he had experienced. The compassion was strong now. I needed to mend his wounds and take this man back into my life. Everyone deserves a second or third chance, and he was not a criminal in my eyes, just a person who had taken an unfortunate path along his road called life.

I did just that—allowed him back into my life. We continued to see each other, although it was a little tense at first and, of course, guarded on my part and his; but this dance would continue as long as I was willing to have my partner take me around my waist and twirl me to another dimension.

The continuation of our dance was preserved with kindness, openness, and greater respect for each other's capabilities on the floor and in life. How we treat other human beings is directly proportional to how we have been treated in life, and to what lessons we learned that were fundamental in creating our personalities and values. Sometimes those lessons are harsh but beneficial. A new and more understanding, compassionate individual emerges, and I felt this was the case for me. The barriers eventually were let down, and a new dance began. We had many conversations that centered on our past experiences and how they shaped us; the ever-present focus for both was understanding each other's patterns in dealing with difficult situations, and how to combat negative responses to those situations that might not be easy to tackle.

Robert Burney writes in *Codependence: The Dance of Wounded Souls*:

> It is through healing our inner child by grieving the wounds that we suffered, that we can change our behavior patterns and clear our emotional process. We can release the grief with our pent up rage, shame, terror, and pain from those feeling places which exist within us. That does not mean that the wounds will ever be completely healed. There will always be a tender spot, a painful place within us due to the experiences that we have had. What it does mean is that we can take the power away from these wounds. By bringing them out of the darkness into the light, by releasing the energy we can heal them enough so that they do not have the power to dictate how we live our lives today. We can heal them enough to change the quality of our lives dramatically. We can heal them enough to truely be happy, Joyous and free in the movement most of the time.

More issues followed, though I suspect that for many people finding themselves in new relationships or in love for the second or third time, preexisting conditions will always be a factor in joining new families. This was one of the obstacles that became a battleground between us.

Difficulties are always inherent in developing new bonds between new partners and existing family members, and the acceptance necessary therein. This is a common problem with second or third relationships. Many children are eager for their parents to move on and be happy, but the reality is that there will always be a distancing from or discord with the new person entering into an already established family. Uncomfortable as it may be to begin with, with time the new presence becomes familiar, expected, and accepted.

The following months seemed to solidify my once-questionable relationship with Mr. Waltz, and the realization that there could be a long-term commitment became anticipated, yet frightening at the same time.

Had enough time and experience with one another passed to make such a commitment? What if little things surfaced that became more significant and bothersome than we thought initially? We were comfortable with one another, yes. But did that mean it should be a lifelong comfort? Would we both carry with us the reservations that led to the demise of our previous relationships: boredom, complacency, lack of trust, taking one another for granted, fear, loss of interest, insecurity, and the like? Our new relationships bear the burdens of the sins of our past. Thoughts of permanence were overshadowed by too many of those sins. Discovery of how strong those ingrained sins were indirectly affected us as dancers. We were to discover that these sins and past themes would prevent us from moving forward.

The first issue with all new dance partners is the same: that person would never live up to what I had in my first and most important family relationship, the family that was created and grew and developed over many years with all the history and memories that goes along with it. This experience cannot be recreated or ever shared as a whole. It can only be added to and embellished once all involved know that the new relationship is not a replacement for what was, only a positive and possibly wonderful addition to what will be in the future. The dance of two individuals in life continues on and off the floor, and only two partners will know for certain if they are suited to be partners for life.

Secondly, dancers must confront differences in the age and stage of life between individual partners. Are they copacetic? The alignment for us was certainly not perfect, neither on solid ground nor within the stars. I was ready for adventure and freedom to move, travel, and enjoy the last third of my life. He had a half a lifetime to finish and would not be at my stage of life until I was of an age that would prohibit me from doing all those things I was ready for now. I couldn't wait. Age wouldn't allow it. The constraints put upon my dance partner due to his past would carry over into the future. He was no longer able to travel outside of the United States. Always checked and rechecked as an offender, he was unable to engage in the now normal social media present in today's world. He couldn't vote or carry a weapon—just a multitude of constant and permanent scars that would affect not only his life, but the lives of those associating with him. Was this fair for all? I thought not. I would be the one to sacrifice a great deal. I wasn't prepared to do this!

A frustration kept resurfacing for me in regard to the give and take between us. Once again, I sensed I was the parent figure and would carry the ills of the child that was lost. If I continued the relationship with Mr. Waltz, I would provide for him emotionally, physically, and financially. It became apparent that I was the one expected to create the experiences for this new family. I would need to invest my resources to keep him interested—travels, dinners, sporting events, managing of his home, and even the lavish gifts that I would have expected my male counterpart would provide for his new love. This was a contradiction in my eyes. I was frustrated that I was providing a great deal more than was getting in return. I was a mother. His mother.

The generation gap presented its own subtle problems. Conversations were limited about events that I had lived through when he was not even born. In discussing the Kennedy assassination, I couldn't help but marvel at how I had lived through that time and the turmoil of the Vietnam War, while he had no concept of what I was feeling. The music of that era was unrecognizable to him, but so vivid and important in shaping who I was. These examples may seem insignificant, but they became so much more significant in the grand scheme of things. Someone once remarked to me that I was the modern-day Mrs. Robinson from the classic movie *The Graduate*. When mentioning this to my youthful counterpart he queried, "Who is Mrs. Robinson?"

There were other instances of a generational disconnect that followed, enough to make me pause and question my decisions about finishing this dance. My childhood memories were very different from his. I remembered games like red light, green light; jumping over the moon; Red Rover; and Captain, may I. I remembered school jokes about cooties, hickeys, and pink belly. We had roller skates that came with keys, and we fashioned our homemade skateboards by using a two-by-four and applying those metal roller skate wheels to the bottom. I had so much fun with toboggan slides, glistening saucers, and bicycles with fat seats, broad fenders, and big tires. We put cards in the spokes to make a sound similar to an automobile's. There was no TV, no Internet in those days. The only phone we had was a party line. If we were lucky we could tap into a neighbor's conversation. We lived in small houses with single baths. Cars were a luxury. Programmed activities were nonexistent. It was a simpler time.

Mr. Waltz and I would never share the familiarity that comes from growing up in the same era, a common thread that weaves our personal experiences into substantive pieces of fabric that are woven into our entire being. Questions about logical decisions filled my head. Could these issues be merely differences, not obstacles in going forward?

> Do we want to choose a partner who is willing to work through issues? If so it can be an incredibly nurturing magical space to explore what true love is- some of the time It cannot be that all of the time. There might be periods of time days weeks even months where things are going beautifully and it seems as though we may have reached happily ever after but then things will change and get different. That is how the life process works It will not be someones fault. It will be a new opportunity for growth for both people who becomes true emotional intimacy (*Codependence,* Burney).

The months to follow showed that there would be little compromising. Many events challenged the once idealistic, loving, romantic couple who seemed to twirl effortlessly on that dance floor but now needed the work to recreate the flow again.

Two years had passed from the beginning of this dance, and lessons and moments of grief had filled the floor with wonder, questions, and doubt. Periods of self-doubt and insecurities continued to be the recurring problem for me. I felt a lack of trust and the inability to defend myself. Constraints we put upon one another and a roller coaster, emotional ride prevented us from continuing our quest for perfection and seemed to block what was once thought to be a wonderful union. Even with all the knowledge gained and handbooks read about relationships and what makes two people whole, too many obstacles seemed to sabotage this once likely couple.

> A healthy romantic relationship is about two whole independent people choosing to become life partners in a life journey for as long as that works for both of them. This

is, of course, a theoretical concept. Because
of the cultural dysfunction and emotional
trauma, all of us have experienced due to the
human condition, we are never in this lifetime going to be completely whole healthy
person with no emotional wounds and we
are never going to meet someone else that
has no emotional wounds (*Codependence*).

Unfortunately, this all looks and sounds ideal on paper, but in reality, so many men and women leave marriages or friendships. People endure for years together as a couple only to discard what they have built over a lifetime as if it is meaningless and unworthy of saving or protecting and cherishing. All that was useful and enjoyable and grown together is forgotten. The couple dissolves like a sugar cube in hot water. Marriages are easily thrown away, as is so much in today's throwaway society. We all start anew. But to what end? Aren't we all a bit apprehensive to begin something that may only end in a similar demise? The fear and brick walls that we build around our emotional selves do not allow for any potential union of two worthy and caring people. The mortar becomes hard and heavy. It is all so scary to face the possible pain of loss once again. Are we all just temporary partners in this dance of life? Just throwaway commodities offering little more than a glimmer of what others may be searching for, but do not really want to find?

This is the phenomenon of the new dating world, particularly for those of us in the third or fourth quarter of our lives. We have already experienced a lot of history in our previous lives, building a new history can feel like just plain too much work.

My dance card is tattered and worn. After attempting many moves with the vast array of dancers out there, I can only conclude that with the human condition come human frailties. With desire and persistence, many will attempt to find that perfect partner, one who will provide all the qualities and attributes that will result in a perfect, mutually respectful, interdependent union. Optimistically, I want to think that kind of partnership is a possibility, but for now, the intellect outweighs the heart. Maybe in time I will fill out a new dance card and begin again.

The years have passed, and my friend is still with her husband of almost 40 years now. Happily? I am not so sure, but they are at least content in their familiarity.

Mr. Contemporary is gone from the dating site. The contemporary dance is one I never practiced, but one I am hopeful to learn one day.

Mr. Slow remains a single man with a very large support system, mostly his immediate family. I still regard him, curiously, as one of my fondest, most genuine partners from the card, and he was my first.

Mr. Tango continues to be that big fish in the bowl of insignificant mediocrity. Mr. Tango, with Ms. Beauty Pageant arm candy, has entered into a questionable monogamous dance. I say questionable because I continue to receive communication every now and then from this unlikely dancer, one I had shrugged off as incorrigible.

Mr. Two-Step disappeared from the virtual world. I envision him not on the farm tinkering with steam tractors anymore. That was a phase. I see him returning to the fast-paced, jet-setting lifestyle of the permanent bachelor he will always be—socially unaware, but content in his solitude.

Mr. Grind is a dancer I will forget and am happy never to have practiced with. I will never practice his form of dance, either.

Mr. Salsa, that one time lovely dance partner for an afternoon of delight remains single. We never reconnected physically to practice this dance, as he is consumed with his art, and creating those beautifully crafted works of art must give him his life's pleasure and meaning. He is alone.

Mr. Rumba and I are in an open relationship. I have a continued connection to this dancer. We have an electrifying bond that will never diffuse. Extreme sports continue to dominate his lifestyle, as well as outside sexual pursuits, no doubt.

Mr. Cha-cha, a solitary sailor, continues to ride the tides, letting the winds in his sails guide his next moves. Noncommittal, we continue our banter on the level of friendship. The dance was a difficult task for him to master. Being on solid ground is not his comfort zone. Gliding along the water's surface is a safe haven for this Cowardly Lion.

Mr. Jitterbug, my antagonistic jitterbug, is left all alone to conquer all those demons. Our reunions are infrequent now. His ever-spinning life does not offer a moment for solitude and reflection on those dance partners who may have provided him with assistance in slowing that wheel of anxiety down. He still remains the cutest dancer on my card and continues to antagonize me sporadically.

Mr. Waltz was my most romantic love partner, and I will carry our relationship with me. I ache for him on occasion but fight within myself, knowing we made the appropriate decision for all. A family of only two, he will be consumed with his daughter's emotional and physical needs in the years to come. I will not offer my expertise. This dancer has moved on, and quickly, I might add. That memorable black fluffy robe still hangs on that hook awaiting the next woman he desires and invites into his hot tub. He will again need to expose his all-too-painful past. I believe he will find that one individual who will be swept away into a fantasy world of impressive rhetoric and intimate splendor, his new sunshine.

As for myself, this introspective journey has been invaluable. It has provided me with the confidence and competence within myself to be who I am and always have been. I have the power to unleash all my talents and accomplishments with full appreciation from others. I want to encourage all the many unrecognized souls who may have forgotten how truly special and deserving they are. Fill out a dance card, create and explore your own personal moves in the hope of finding a meaningful, life-fulfilling discovery.

My dance card will remain locked away. Forever? Probably not. Never say never. I will someday receive those boots that will bring me back to that dance floor of love.

About the Author

Ann is a resident of Wisconsin. She earned her Bachelor of Science degree in Education and in Nursing. She worked as an orthopedic nurse and public health nurse in both hospital and clinical settings. After retirement she returned to her creative passions: drawing, painting, illustrating for children's and poetry books. Writing became a natural progression. Ann has two adult daughters that have encouraged her in every aspect of this adventure.

Her love of sports began early in her life and she enjoys skiing, skating tennis, golf, water sports, football, basketball and biking. Along with her athletic endeavors she has been seen on stage in regional and theatrical performances. Singing is predominant theme, and performing as a family is a passion. Passion for the ones we love and productivity in the life we live creates balance and happiness, a personal motivation she hopes will be obtained by those in her life